Songs of Seas and Stars

Madeline Dau R.A. Krueger
Chelsea M. Brown Katharine Bost

Songs of Seas and Stars

Madeline Dau R.A. Krueger
Chelsea M. Brown Katharine Bost

Kaleidoscope

First paperback edition July 2023

Book cover designed by Taylor at Sweet 15 Designs
Interior book layout designed by CMB Editing
Interior images designed by R.A. Krueger

ISBN 978-1-961114-01-2 (paperback)
ISBN 978-1-961114-00-5 (eBook)

Published by the Kaleidoscope Author Co-op
facebook.com/groups/kaleidoscopeauthors

Table of Contents

Kaleidoscope
Powerful Women
Powerful Writers
Powerful Words

Introduction

Welcome to the Kaleidoscope Co-op. We are a group of authors who love weaving words into stories, from the familiar to the fantastical. Our goal is to publish two anthologies per year, featuring stories with strong and engaging characters. We aim to build a community promoting women writers and discussions about the craft of writing.

Our first collection, *Songs of Seas and Stars*, features four original stories tied together with the common threads of mermaids and pearls along with a theme of opposites.

 @KaleidoscopCoOp   facebook.com/kaleidoscopeauthors

 @KaleidoscopeCoOp   @KaleidoscopeCoOp

i

Veydra's Eye

Madeline Dau

Daughter dearest, Daughter mine,
Would you recast the grasp of time,
Revive a life or make wrongs right,
If Veydra's power lay in sight?
But Her Eye won't open for just any.
To be worthy of the Sea Mother's gaze,
Pay in full the tithe of red tides,
Cleansed by iron, sanctified in salt.
We await you above the Silent Maw,
Where you must fall to fly.

– Gorgonas' Hymn

Rain pelts the silent crowd gathered on the grand outdoor staircase leading up to the castle. Old women and men and children stand like granite sculptures, heads bowed. Merys doesn't notice the icy rivulets wending down her cheeks and beneath her collar—she only has eyes for the box on its pedestal. In the downpour, water collects in the two-tailed gorgona mermaid carving and the glossy white paint glistens like diamonds.

Just like the ones embedded in Queen Avyria's crown.

Her mother's crown presses on Merys's scalp, so much heavier than her own, or rather, the one that was hers this morning. Furtive glances steal at her profile. Curious castleguards, concerned brothers. Wet and shivering citysfolk, considered too weak to fight in the war yet hale enough to supply an entire army with food and weapons.

And stand in the bone-chilling rain for a queen's funeral.

Merys knows she must speak. She must say something to the people gathered in the gloom. But she can't tear her gaze away from the polished white box, latched tight against the rain. If it were sunny, the lid would be thrown open, revealing a last look at the lovely queen in repose. At least, she was lovely once—the sickness took her slowly, her muscles wasting away so her skin cinched around her bones like leathery corsets. The garish cosmetics the undertaker applied to the queen's shriveled countenance resemble stagecraft.

Perhaps it's best the lid is closed.

Merys's eldest brother, Ephraim, clears his throat.

"I…" Merys stammers. Her voice trembles as much as her lips. She twists her fingers together, as if that will wring the eulogy into existence.

Her brother closest in companionship and age, Reyvain, rests a hand on her shoulder, but that doesn't shield her from Ephraim's impatient gesture.

"I'm sorry, I can't—" Merys claps a hand over her mouth and stumbles away from the top of the stairs and into the castle.

No one shouts for her to return or gives chase to drag her back—that would be uncouth at the best of times, let alone a royal funeral. Merys trips over her hem, nearly spilling to the floor. With a strangled cry, she braces a hand against the wall and kicks free of the flimsy heeled slippers.

Though she's inside, water still dribbles down her cheeks. She swipes a burning eye with the back of her hand. The onslaught of tears keeps coming just like the rain. The halls are empty aside from their sconces and tapestries—everyone is outside. Staring at a white box.

But staring won't bring her back.

If it would, Merys would never blink again—if unblinking contact was all it took to hear her mother's voice, she would cut her eyelids away and stare at that box with its motionless contents until she died herself.

Merys pads through the corridors in a daze, the stone cold against her bare feet. She finds herself on the threshold of her mother's favorite room: the library. Lightning illuminates the dim interior. Thunder follows, rattling the floor-to-ceiling bay window embracing the reading nook. Blinking away the harsh afterimage seared into her eyes, Merys ventures inside.

Bookshelves cover the two-story walls, accessible by stairs, balconies, and, for the brave, by spindly little ladders. The royal collection includes a little of everything—studies of economics, applications of engineering, architecture, medicine. Queen Avyria always lamented the dearth of literature. Craning her neck at the packed shelves, Merys can't imagine how her mother had time to read them all. But she had, or at least she claimed to have. It was why she was always smuggling books into the castle and stashing them wherever she could find room. Inside the massive old clock is—was—her favorite.

Merys trails her fingers along the spines as she wanders from the section on arcane religious texts to the atlases. Mother's latest project is scattered all over the reading nook—a sprawling sea tour to follow the route of one of her favorite historical plays. A dream for the peace following the bloody war with Gravehold. Something hopeful to look forward to, to help them forget about her illness.

Everything burns through Merys at once— the cruel injustice that her mother was taken from her, hatred for her mother's disease, shame for her inability to lead the mourning rites in front of the crowd. A shriek tears her throat as she yanks a dusty book from the shelf. She hurls it at the wall. The pages rustle as they float to the floor. It doesn't make her feel better, but she can't stop. She is a ragdoll clamped within rage's feral jaws—shaken and battered and helpless. She throws another book. And another. If there is anything that will claw the Queen of Kaleirusia from the Warden of Death's clutches, it is damaging her precious library. She would never stand for it—she'd snapped at Merys's siblings more than once for even considering entering the library with food or drink. Merys will destroy every book in this room if she must.

"Merys!" Reyvain snatches her arm as she draws back to throw

Tethys's Isles: A Sailor's Almanac. "Stop!"

The book tumbles through her fingers, landing with a heavy thud. Reyvain clutches her to his chest, his heartbeat drumming against her ear. She struggles against arms like iron bands, howling at the unoccupied shelf. The rectangle of empty space gapes like a wound, one Merys can't stop picking.

Mother should have come by now. If she was ever going to, she would have done so already. Storms and squalls, the queen is really and truly dead.

"I know, Mer," Reyvain says into her hair. "I know."

Tears come again, hot and shameful. Merys buries her face in her brother's crushed brocade tunic. The soft material rubs against her forehead. Her tears join the sodden mess on his shirtfront. After what seems like hours, Merys lifts her head, sniffling.

"I don't know what to do. I'm not ready to lead a queendom—not through peaceful times, let alone war." She chokes back another sob, biting her lip in the process. "If Mother couldn't turn the tide, what am *I* going to do?"

"You're not alone," Reyvain replies. "You have nine older brothers, and none of us will let anything happen to you."

Merys shakes her head and hiccups. "I'm not worried about me. I'm worried about the people—how they deserve…"

"I know." Reyvain sighs, draping his arm around her shoulders. He smells like pine and woodsmoke. "Let's clean this up, Mer."

Together, they return the books to the shelves. Most are unscathed, but a few have broken spines, and they must hunt for loose pages missing from an old gorgona prayer book honoring Veydra, the Sea Mother. Merys's stomach aches with the sick twist of guilt. This was not how a princess—a queen—was supposed to behave.

Reyvain places a heavy volume on the shelf on his way to the alcove with Mother's itinerary. Merys joins him at the low glass table, sinking into the soft cushions indented by years of her mother's sitting. Sheaves of parchment with Mother's pristine handwriting lay in messy stacks. Her water lily perfume lingers like a memory of incense. Merys sighs and stares up at the large painting across from her. A life-sized portrait depicts her ancestor, warrior Queen Asha, unbending in heavy armor. So great, she was considered a demigoddess serving Veydra and inspired more than a few cults over the years. Mother liked to joke that the way to end the war was to consider "what would great Aunt Asha do?"

Sitting in Mother's chair, staring at the painting, a dull pain gnaws through Merys's stomach up through her chest. She is undeserving of this place, unfit to rule Kaleirusia. The tidal chart maps and itineraries blur through her tears as she organizes the loose pages.

Reyvain's lips move as he reads a piece of parchment to himself. "Mother was always enamored with Veydra's exploits." He sets the slim playbook praising the sea goddess's cunning and bravery on top of Merys's pile.

Merys can hardly bear to look at it—the gilded cover with stamped letters dredges memories of hours spent listening to her mother read the script aloud.

"I had a feeling I'd find you here," Ephraim says, gliding into the library.

Merys jolts upright and skirts around the table. Ephraim's once gentle face hides behind a carefully cultivated beard. Twenty years Merys's senior, he is a more present father than the general king has ever been. But that makes him more of a parent than a brother, more parent than friend.

"Merys..." Ephraim sighs, dragging a hand down his forehead. "With Mother dead, you're going to have to navigate uncomfortable situations sometimes."

"I know," Merys mumbles to the floor.

"You're the queen. No more hiding beneath tablecloths at banquets. You'll have to direct the army and send people to their deaths to protect the many, marry a stranger to ensure our family's future..."

"I know that!" Tears burn Merys's eyes. "I've been preparing for a political alignment for my entire life. But talking about Mother to that crowd of people...like she's gone..."

Ephraim rests a hand on her shoulder. "Mer...she *is* gone. I know as the youngest and only daughter, you two were inseparable. But you're sixteen now. It's time to—"

Captain Galehaven blusters into the library, face like a tomato beneath his coarse brown whiskers. "My liege—urgent news from the front!" His shiny black boots punish the tiles as he crosses the room and thrusts a letter at Merys. She blinks, tears clinging to her lashes. Her brothers exchange a glance. Ephraim takes the letter while Reyvain wraps a steady arm around her shoulders. Merys cringes closer to her brother as four other castleguards storm the room, boots clanking against the floor. She wanted to scream at them to leave, to get out of her mother's sanctuary.

The eldest prince picks at the wax seal, frowning. "You've read it?"

"Yes, milord. I didn't want to disturb your day of mourning, but I'm afraid this cannot wait."

Ephraim unfolds the heavy parchment, gray eyes darting along the lines of code. Merys inches closer. The front—does the captain refer to the front lines? That's where her father is, leading the army against Gravehold. The letter slips from Ephraim's fingers. Merys dives from Reyvain's safe embrace to catch it before it hits the ground. She parses through the alchemical symbols and glyphs. Mother taught her military codes along with her numbers and letters.

Army routed at Baltric's Fissure
General King Reichard captured

Merys's legs crumple beneath her, knees slamming into the hard floor. Two parents gone in one day.

"What are your orders, my liege?"

There is no measure or scale for the weight of gazes pressing down on Merys's shoulders. The paper crinkles in her grip, rustling like leaves in the wind. She stares up at the others from the ground.

"I—" Her throat feels like she has swallowed a mouthful of sand. The room swims at the edges of her vision, shadows pressing in like thumbs against her eyes. The silence in the library jabs her eardrums like icepicks.

"Summon the councilors to the war room," Ephraim says. "The Queen shall join us shortly."

As the castleguards file from the room, Reyvain stoops to pull Merys to her feet. She overhears harsh murmurs fading in the hall. Perhaps they're discussing her father's predicament.

Or perhaps they're discussing how unfit she is to rule.

"Now is not the time to show weakness." Ephraim draws his cloak tighter. "Steel yourself for the next hours, sister, and we can grieve tonight."

"Ephraim is the acting royal general now," Reyvain says after the eldest prince vanishes into the hallway. "You won't be alone. If you're afraid, the general can manage the room."

Merys nods, biting her lip. Her mother would be so ashamed— she'd spent years guiding and molding her into a capable ruler, and now Merys can't even find her voice. She knows she can rely on her brother, but what use is a queen to her queendom if she's too scared to speak or act?

"Can you come too?" She despises how small her voice sounds.

"Of course, if you wish."

"Tell them I'll just be another minute."

He frowns, weighing his words. "Take your time, Mer. You're the queen—you rush for no one."

The void left behind after Reyvain departs for the war room feels like a cloak made of ice. A physical thing to shy away from rather than a mere absence. Merys shivers, rubbing warmth into her arms. Something rustles beneath her bare foot. An aged piece of vellum peeks between her toes. Frowning, she crouches to pick it up. She and Reyvain must have missed a page from one of the books. A new wave of shame washes over her. Her country needs her to lead, to be strong, and all she has accomplished today is ruin a few of her mother's favorite possessions.

She smooths the page flat with shaking fingers. It's fragment from the playbook—the scenes detailing the Sacrifice of Veydra's Eye. Mother's favorite part of the story. The warrior goddess of the sea and her allies were losing a battle with the sky. When her wife, Terris, fell beneath the sky god's twin blades of lightning and wind, Veydra plucked her right eye free and sacrificed it to Baltric, Warden of Death. He released Terris from his crypts and together they defeated the sky and fortified their realms.

Mother always surmised the myth is real, that Veydra's eye is somewhere out in the world and grants wishes.

If only it wasn't a story. If only.

Merys folds the page in half and tucks it into her sash, where it rests flush against her waist.

When Merys finally reaches the war room, her small throne at the head of the table is the only seat unoccupied. Reyvain notices her first, from his chair at her throne's right, and stands. Everyone else takes note, and suddenly Merys's vision shifts from the tops of heads and elaborate braids to a sea of coats and dresses, all varying degrees of drenched from the rainy vigil. Merys wipes her palms against her bodice as she trudges to her elevated chair. She forgot to put her shoes back on. There's enough murmuring that no one should hear her bare feet slapping against the stone. She perches on her throne, ready to bolt, and the rest of the room sits all at once.

All Merys must do is consider the advice of her council. She can do that. She won't even have to speak much. She forces a weary smile to her lips. "Thank you all for coming on such short notice."

The people surrounding the table rumble in assent.

"By now, you might have heard that the General King has been captured by Gravehold's army," Captain Galehaven says.

"General," Ephraim corrects. "His queen has passed away."

The captain of the castleguards scoffs. "The princess hasn't been coronated."

Merys wishes she could slide from her throne and curl out of sight beneath the table. Her stomach churns like the ocean in a maelstrom, battering at her diaphragm.

"We can officially coronate Queen Merys tonight—I speak on behalf of my brothers and kin, there is no need to dissect logistics of succession." Ephraim's gaze cuts through the gathering like a knife, brooking no opposition. He has trained for his duty to Merys's crown since he could hold a wooden sword.

A coronation ceremony. Not another thing to plan. Hidden by the cover of the table, Merys slips her mother's favorite myth from her sash. She has to take control of the room, before Captain Galehaven undermines her even more. Reyvain nudges her knee reassuringly.

"We'll send for the clerics after the funeral rites are finished tonight?" Merys's voice catches the end like a question. She smothers a cringe at how childish she sounds.

Ephraim nods definitively. "Now, for the reason we're all here. The General has been captured. Any ransom demands?"

The Councilor of Security shakes her head. "No, and the Graveholders have responded with hostility to any and all communication attempts since the beginning of the war. My tentative recommendation is to try to take him back, either directly or through subterfuge."

"Without the general, our army stands no chance against their cavalry," Reyvain says. "If we can draw them to the sea, our navy has the advantage."

The Captain and Councilor of Security exchange a glance.

"And what, exactly, would you know about it?" Captain Galehaven sits back and crosses his arms over his barrel chest. "You're not even on the Council. Let the Councilor of Commerce and Sails determine how best to utilize our navy."

Color flushes Reyvain's face. The older princes and aunts and uncles living in the queendom hold the prestigious councilor positions. Despite their mother's influence, the youngest of her nine sons was always relegated to minor roles in the Arena of Politicos, even as inelegant as studying crops in Regalia.

The Councilor of Commerce and Sails, Merys's great uncle and the captain's longtime drinking partner, clears his throat with a nervous cough. "Naturally. Historically, Kaleirusia has always had the superior navy."

And historically the Queens of Kaleirusia took the helm from Uncle Horstaff and his predecessors and led the navy themselves. Merys rubs the parchment between her thumbs and fingertips beneath the table. Could they possibly expect her to lead ships into battle like her mother?

Without warning, the heavy wooden door shrieks on its hinges and bounces against the wall. A harried courier scrambles into the war room, sweat plastering her hair to her forehead. Her wild, brown eyes sweep the room, landing on Merys. She darts to the young queen's side and stumbles through an awkward bow, clutching her ribs and panting. "Your Resplendence! Word from the High Magus of Gravehold!"

Merys tucks the worn paper story back into her sash and takes the letter. It weighs more than she expected.

"That will be all," Ephraim says.

The courier bows again and runs from the room. Merys's hands tremble so that she nearly drops the letter. The thick, heavy paper made from Gravehold's iron pines reeks, pungent with resin. And decay. Odd. The wax seal cracks beneath her fingers, spilling burgundy crumbles into her lap. Something light tumbles from the folded paper onto the table.

A single finger ending with a charred stump.

Merys shrieks and jumps from her seat, dislodging Mother's— her—crown. The heavy driftwood throne does not budge, and she falls against the table, catching herself inches above the mutilated digit. Father's signet ring glints in the lamplight, caught snug between the cauterized nub and the first knuckle.

Bile creeps up her throat. Someone is shouting, but she can hardly hear anything over the blood roaring in her ears. She pushes against the table, the solid surface the only tether to the earth. Ephraim is shouting for the courier while Reyvain sweeps the finger into a handkerchief. Slowly, Merys looks down at the letter quivering between her shaking fingers.

Resplendent Merys,

Doubtless by now, you have been informed of your father's fate. He is comfortable in Gravehold's Iron Fortress. Not to worry, my Inquisitors are taking the utmost care of him. He sends his regards. And his ring, in case you doubt my hospitality.

You'll want him returned to you with all haste, I'm sure. Be assured, I'm happy to share my demands. All I require is your hand.

Merys glances at the lump cradled in Reyvain's hands, hidden behind white linen. Tears blur her vision as she returns to the letter.

Not literally, although I'm sure you'll think otherwise upon receiving my enclosed gift. No, I propose a marriage alliance. I grow weary of this unending war, sniping at each other generation after generation. I hope you'll accept my offer. I'll continue sending your father's body parts until you do.

Ever yours,
Ferryn Scarforger, Eighth of His Name
King of Gravehold, High Magus, Lord of the Broken Spine Mountains

"What does it say?" Ephraim asks. "Is it a ransom?"

Merys nods, dazed. She barely feels the paper slip through her fingers as her brother seizes it.

More body parts? Does the king of Gravehold really intend to send her father home one finger at a time?

Merys leans against the table, blinking against the gray spots swirling in her vision. She traces the maze of whorls in the wooden grains to ground herself.

"What do they want?" the Security Councilor demands.

"Merys." Ephraim lowers the letter. "He wants Merys."

"In exchange for the general?"

"And a truce." Ephraim stare bores into her.

"A truce? We must take it!" the Councilor of Commerce and Sails says. "They've cut off our access to the northern trade routes, and with winter approaching, we'll starve—"

"Have you lost your wits, Horstaff?" The Councilor of Security slams her fists into the table. "Gravehold means to absorb Kaleirusia! And you just want to deliver our country to that bloody tyrant on a golden plate?"

Uncle Horstaff clenches his jaw, wringing his fingers. "We don't know that's what he intends."

"Why else would he want the princess—I mean queen?" she replies. "I've read reports regarding Scarforger's fear tactics for keeping his subjects quiet and docile that would make you want to gouge your eyes out. Can you imagine how catastrophic his rule would be? If you crave his kingship so much, I invite you to move to his new conquests. Regalia and Kiyoshi have no shortage of empty houses, what with all of the torture and murder."

"But we must do something about supplies," Uncle Horstaff whines. "We can't risk a siege during winter."

"It's recently come to my attention that you're the Councilor of Commerce of a seafaring nation," Reyvain says dryly. "Perhaps you can figure out how best to utilize the fisheries and our trade partners?"

"Watch your tongue, boy—"

"In any case, Merys should decide," Reyvain adds. "She's the queen."

"I—I need to think," Merys stammers, shuddering under the weight of the room's tense stares. Bracing her palm on the table, she starts toward the door.

"Er—Your Resplendence, aren't you forgetting something?" the Councilor of Security asks.

Merys tenses, mind racing. The Councilor lifts the jeweled crown from the floor. Merys's hand flies to her hair, as if there may be more than one diamond and pearl concoction and surely the Councilor is holding a shoddy replica.

But her head is bare. Merys remembers the crown falling when she opened Gravehold's letter with an unpleasant jolt. How her mother's treasure plinked against the table and onto the stone floor before rolling out of sight.

"My thanks," she mutters, snatching it from the woman's hands and running from the room. Ephraim calls for her to wait, but she doesn't stop until she reaches her bedroom.

Merys slams the heavy walnut door behind her and throws her back against the carved wood, chest heaving. Without looking, she fumbles for the iron key jutting from the lock and wrenches. The bolt sliding home echoes in her empty room.

The servants must have moved most of her belongings to the queen's quarters. Now she doesn't even have a familiar refuge in which to recover. The bare bones of the room—furniture and mirrors—remain, but anything personal is gone. No sheets or tapestries or clothes. She shuffles across the room toward her bare bed. Her reflection in the tall standing mirror flickers in her peripheral vision like a ghost.

The girl in the glass flinches, face pale. She looks like a child playing dress up. Trying on her mother's jewelry and dresses. Merys inches closer, brushing the cold surface with her fingertips. Her breath fogs the glass. This girl doesn't look like a queen of Kaleirusia. Like someone took the essence of Warrior Queen Asha's portrait in the library and diluted it with all the water in the sixteen seas.

The crown perched on her head looks as unsettling and heavy as it feels. It doesn't belong on her head. Maybe it never will. Merys swipes a hand beneath her eyes, drying her cheeks. The jewels flash with each small movement. The massive central pearl resembles an opalescent moon, shuddering with the palest lilacs, rose quartzes, and ivory depending on the gloomy half-light infiltrating the window.

A wave of pearly white glints from the top of the pearl to the bottom and recedes, leaving a burnished gold circle in its wake. Merys furiously blinks away the tears to clear her vision. It was a trick of the light. The lighting is terrible, especially with the dreary rain—

The pearl appears to blink again.

Merys jerks away from the mirror. Her reflection doesn't quite follow suit, her face eerily calm as she steps back. She yanks the crown from her head, nearly dropping it in her haste to turn it so that strange pearl faces up.

It appears normal. An ordinary pearl, surrounded by glittering platinum. Merys tilts the crown to better catch the light. There it is again—the colors swirl like silt in a lazy current. The golden circle resembles a whirlpool now, a black vortex dragging the threads of rich caramel into a pit so dark, Merys forgets to breathe. It's a void-black pupil surrounded by a golden iris. But Merys has seen this gorgeous but ordinary pearl nearly every day for her entire life.

And yet, it is undeniable an eye.

"Veydra's…Eye?"

The white sheet undulates, and the darker colors vanish, leaving the pearl the pale cream of old bone. No matter how she turns it, Merys can't find the Eye again. She couldn't have imagined it—sweat plasters her dress to the backs of her legs, and her stomach feels like it's trying to crawl up her throat. She prods her belly with a grimace.

Paper crinkles beneath her fingers.

Merys sinks to her knees, reverently freeing the page from her sash. In the myth, Veydra wished on her own eye to restore a loved one from death. Her eyes drink the words like a sailor lost at sea without water. She clutches the crown like a mast in the storm.

"Please… please bring her back," she whispers, lips brushing against the jewel.

The room is silent aside from her ragged breathing. Did it work?

Merys stumbles to her feet and darts to the window. The white box remains still on its plinth. She stares at the coffin, muttering fervid prayers as the tines of the crown bite into her palms.

But nothing happens. An uneasy laugh wells up, filling the room and dissolving into gasping sobs. It's ridiculous, but Merys feels the empty rip of losing her mother all over again. She rests her forehead on the windowsill, cursing herself and the winds and the gods in between hiccups.

Something tickles her ear. Thin, dry lips whisper the melody of the ocean—the waves shushing against the sand, crashing against rocks. She jerks up, nearly bashing her forehead against the window.

The pearl blinks to ivory blankness again.

It's real. She's not imagining it. No matter how she turns the crown, she can't elicit the blink or the sound of the ocean again, she can't prove it to herself, but there is no other explanation.

Then why doesn't it work?

Merys scours through the myth again. Ah. Veydra had to travel to the Silent Maw, an odd isle jutting from the ocean that connects all three realms—earth, water, and sky.

And Mother had charted a course passing this monument as she was dying.

This is fate—this war has been dragging on for years. It's no coincidence that Scarforger made such a move now, or that Mother had determined the exact voyage outlined in this divine play, or that a goddess's eye has been hiding in plain sight for hundreds of years. The winds of the universe are herding her toward inevitable purpose: avoid the clutches of Ferryn Scarforger and resurrect Queen Avyria. If she moves quickly, she'll return the true Queen to her throne before her people can suffer for her flight.

Merys's hushed breath fogs the window, obscuring her features. Through the mist, the girl in the window resembles Queen Avyria more than Merys ever has. She'll do it—she'll follow her mother's sea charts.

In the dim quiet of evening and nighttime, Merys's preparations go unnoticed. After prying Veydra's Eye from its setting with a plain iron nail file, she sneaks to the library to grab her mother's sea charts. Quiet as the tide, she slips through the castle to the docks tucked within the protection of the castle's ground floor.

Queen Avyria's single-sail dinghy bobs in the water. By far the smallest and most distinctive vessel in the fleet, it's the only one she can maneuver alone. She steels herself and clambers into the boat. The sail, tension in the ropes, reaction of the rudder all seem to be in perfect working order. It has been months since Mother was well enough to take to the seas, but Merys's fingers remember the equipment like her lungs remember to breathe. Before she can change her mind, she unties the boat from its moorings and pushes into the dark lagoon beneath the castle.

Normally, her mother would have a dockhand tow them into the sea with a rope to avoid rowing. Anxious to avoid notifying the dockmasters, Merys grabs the oars. Her shoulders burn after a few strokes. The smooth wood rubs against her hands, and she can already feel where blisters will bubble through her skin.

A flickering light burns away the gloom ahead. Merys swallows against the tightening in her throat. The Salt Portcullis—she'd forgotten all about it, the gate that blocks the lagoon's exit to the sea. She stares despairingly at the sides of the boat. How was she going to moor her boat, climb the steep ledge to the chain house, and raise the bars, all without the guards noticing?

Merys holds the oars aloft as the boat drifts closer to the light. A lantern flickers on the raised walkway, nestled between a sturdy boot and a green bottle rocking on its side. A castleguard slumps in his chair, chin resting on his chest. His snores echo off the stone walls and high stone ceiling.

She should be furious that the man guarding the weakest point of the castle is sleeping, but she can't help but feel that Veydra is looking out for her. As quietly as she can, she paddles beneath the sleeping guard, closer to the chain house.

But the portcullis has already been raised. Nerves twist her stomach like the coils of a black-diamond sea snake. Her boat drifts beneath the iron spikes and their raiment of barnacles. Briny water plinks onto her head and shoulders, and she shudders from the cold.

A pair of small fishing vessels bob in the darkness outside the castle, lashed together with rope. Divers searching for luminescent pearls in the deep dark. Fearful of being recognized by the two-tailed gorgona mermaid on her sail, Merys rows harder. Muscles in her legs, arms, and back smolder with pain. As she glides past, voices drift by her, snatched away by the wind.

A tiny voice in the deep recesses of her mind whispers, asking if she's sure she knows what she's doing. It sounds like the dour, old Councilors. Like the people who have whispered behind her back for the last ten years about how she didn't have enough steel to follow Queen Avyria.

The sail snaps, and the dinghy jolts forward. Smiling tentatively, Merys tucks the oars away and stands. Here, she is closest to her mother—balancing on a few inches of wood in the midst of the sea goddess. Her hand delves into her pocket. Veydra's Eye warms her skin like sunlight. She finds her bearings and adjusts her course, angling the prow toward the inky horizon beneath Terris's constellation twinkling high above.

By the fifth day of sailing, Merys has the sea charts memorized. She disregarded the first week of Mother's voyage to Tethys's Isles, aiming straight for the Silent Maw. Thick, gray clouds trudge through the heavens, hiding the sun and its piercing glare. Merys squints at the horizon. A needle pierces through the cerulean of the ocean to the pale blue stratified with clouds.

She licks her cracked, salty lips. The only thing she regrets not packing is her small tin of beeswax, but she didn't want to risk venturing to the queen's quarters to look for it among her missing possessions. But it doesn't matter now, she muses as she sips lukewarm water from the skin stashed in the ship's tiny hold. She'll make landfall tonight, and with the full moon, she might even be able to find where to make her wish so that the Sea Mother can hear. Then Mother will be restored, and everything will mend itself. Twisting, she turns her face to the wind at her back, sighing as the gusts drag their fingers through her hair. An acrid tendril of smoke tickles her nose. Her eyes snap open.

Her mind can't interpret what she sees. A schooner boasting three masts and at least ten sails blots the horizon behind her. Kaleirusian made but rather than her country's royal blue ship cresting a wave above a gorgona, its banner bears a silver hand grasping at an arc of three stars on an ink black background.

Gravehold's banner.

Despite the heat and salt, Merys's blood runs cold in her veins. How did a Gravehold banner find its way onto a Kaleirusian ship? And what are the odds that it's a half-day behind her, bearing in the same direction when no trade routes run this way? Her gaze sweeps over her lone sail, the royal emblem pulled taught on white canvas. The gorgona stares blankly skyward, twin fish tails coiled together. She has never wanted to hide her country's emblem before, but if she's close enough to smell the smoke emanating from the other ship, it's close enough to see her sail. And no other ships moored in their lagoon are permitted to bear the Kaleirusian crest *directly* on the sails rather than flags.

Wind whips Merys's hair as she flings herself to the labyrinth of ropes. She makes minute adjustments with her sail trim, taking advantage of every minute shift in the wind. The smudge on the horizon behind her looms ever closer, faster than the towering Maw ahead. She tries not to think about how Gravehold apprehended her country's ship or what will happen if they catch her. Each desperate gasp and struggling heartbeat drag for an eternity.

Hours pass, the clouds devouring the sunlight. The first raindrop hits her cheek like a slap. The sky above unleashes a torrent of water, as if the Sea Mother and Sky Father are at war as they were in ancient times.

The shore is just ahead, the Silent Maw rising above like a pillar supporting the sky. The sea charts detail a meandering path, but with the sand in sight and the ship close enough to hear shouting from the men aboard, Merys forges straight. It's a temporary solution, but she can hide amidst the Maw's foothills.

Lightning illuminates a jagged rock stabbing through the roiling water. Merys yanks the rudder, shoulder screaming with strain. The dinghy jerks to the right, skirting around the obsidian dark stone. Something rakes against the bottom of her boat, nearly dragging her to a halt. The rudder catches something beneath the waves and snaps like bone.

Merys shrieks as the small vessel skids sideways and tilts, drenching her with seawater. She scrambles for something else to hold onto and narrowly remains aboard. Without the rudder, the dinghy careens into another obsidian rock. There must be a reef hidden just beneath the waves. She'll never make it to the shore in the boat by chance.

She tumbles from the boat, gritting her teeth against the icy water seeping into her clothes. The sodden fabric pulls her face beneath the surface of the water. She flails, scrabbling at the reef for purchase. The rock slices her palm like broken glass, but she manages to hoist herself onto the ledge of jagged stone. Her perch is a few feet wide, submerged beneath a few inches of water.

A massive shadow turns the already dimmed light to night. The Kaleirusian schooner crashes into the labyrinth of stone. Ship beams splinter like kindling. Sailors' shouts are lost in the roiling thunder of shattering wood as the treacherous rocks rend the hull.

Merys stands on the reef, wobbling as she shuffles toward the shore. Her dress writhes around her ankles as if alive. She reaches the edge and jumps, swimming to the next sharp, black barrier. She hardly manages to climb up onto the treacherous reef when something snags her hair and twists. She falls back against a barreled chest and a coarse beard that scratches the back of her neck.

"That's far enough, chit." The sailor's breath reeks of rum and tooth decay.

"Let go!" Merys claws at the leathery hand tangled in her hair. Salt and pain burn her eyes.

"King's orders. You don't come, we don't get paid."

"In what vessel do you plan to deliver me?" Merys snaps, braver than she feels. "Your ship is ruined!"

"I'll row you to Gravehold myself if I have to." He shakes her, and Merys loses her footing and falls to her knees. The unforgiving stone slices through her dress.

"I'm the queen of Kaleirusia." Merys grunts in pain. More sailors are swimming through the stone labyrinth's trenches. She'll never escape now. "Whatever Ferryn Scarforger is paying you, I can double it."

"It's not just about the money, chit," the sailor admits. "It's also about not having my limbs hacked from my body."

Something slender and green snakes from the water and cinches around the man's ankle. It yanks, and he falls on his stomach next to Merys. He groans dully before jerking up, an expression of agony and terror cutting through the daze. He opens his mouth, emptying his lungs in the most horrific scream. Merys claps her palms over her ears, but it doesn't muffle the sudden chorus of shrieks.

All across the warren of hidden stone, grizzled men and women plunge beneath the water as if weighted by anchors. Some splash back to the surface, shouting and pleading with the Sea Mother before vanishing beneath the waves again.

The sailor next to Merys loses consciousness and collapses face first into the shallow water concealing their ledge. Merys gasps, instinctively reaching to roll him to his back. The man's beard billows like seaweed, and blood coats the inside of his nostrils. His boot bobs to the surface, trailing a tail of sinew and ragged flesh.

Merys shrieks and releases him. He drifts toward the shore, the rocks scraping along his back, before something wrenches him underwater by his hair. The water beside Merys churns like boiling water. Something erupts from the chaos, showering her with seawater.

A woman braces her arms against the ledge, everything below her waist submerged. Her skin is the pale green of shallow water over seaweed. Water streams from her violet hair, dribbling over her bare chest. She grins, revealing a shark's blood-stained teeth. Rusty liquid drips from the gills lining her neck.

"Shore Daughter," the not-woman rasps, her voice iron and salt. Twin scaled tails curl lazily from the water. A gorgona, a rarity even this far from human cities. "My sisters and I accept your generous offering."

Merys shudders, lips working soundlessly. Her limbs refuse to respond to simple commands—scooting backward along the rock, diving into the water. Fleeing for the shore. The gorgona reaches for her, cupping her cheek with a cold palm. The gossamer webbing between the gorgona's fingers sticks to her skin. The creature wipes her palm from Merys's cheek and across her mouth.

The stench and taste of iron and salt and bile burns her eyes. Merys gags and flinches away. She rubs her lips, hands shaking, and her fingertips come away bloody. Whose blood? The sailor's?

The gorgona smiles again, rows of teeth meshing together like a steel trap. "The way is open to you, Shore Daughter."

Merys whimpers and scoots backward. Her palm presses on nothing, and she tumbles into the ocean. She twists and fights to the surface, feet lashing against her skirts. When her head breaks the water, the gorgona has vanished. Merys swims for the shore, clambering over the rocks and cringing whenever something large and slick glances off her legs. Her muscles and lungs burn by the time she crawls onto the beach. Sand clings to the ragged cuts dissecting her palms.

She glances back over her shoulder.

Mother's dinghy is a pile of splintered toothpicks washing up farther down the beach. Waves devour the halves of the Kaleirusian ship as flames lick the masts and Gravehold's flag. Occasional flashes of lightning illuminate the red-tinged waves and tails curling above the water. A few sailors splash frantically toward the shore, more interested in escaping the gorgonas than capturing her.

Swiping sweat and salt from her eyes with the back of her forearm, Merys presses to her feet and runs across the sand to the safety of the foothills. The fine grains infiltrate her shoes, rubbing her heels raw. She scrambles up sheer rockfaces, leaving scarlet palm prints behind. Lightning illuminates a cave mouth, and she darts inside. She feels her way through the dark, scraping her hands against the walls.

A milky light infiltrates the gloom. Panting, Merys trudges toward it. Her sodden dress and shoes weigh as much as a mountain. She passes beneath the light, a sconce caging a luminescent pearl the size of her fist.

There is another ahead.

The ground shifts from sand to uneven pebbles to smooth, delicate tiles. The narrow passage opens into a large cavern. Gilded pillars support the high ceiling, carved with waves and clouds. Luminescent pearls cast each pillar in ghostly light. Across the open space, a coiled staircase waits beyond a high archway. The floor mosaic forms a glossy portrait of the Trinity: Earth, Sea, and Sky. Merys's breath catches in her chest. The Silent Maw is a temple, and she is here to make an offering.

She delves into her pocket for Veydra's Eye, wincing as the stiff fabric rubs against her hands. Her palms resemble a gutted fish from climbing over the obsidian reefs. She combs the cavern, searching for an alcove or an altar, but something diverts her attention. Her hair snaps against her cheeks as she turns her head. It's not her imagination—heavy boots crunch over the cave tunnel's rocky floor, heading for her.

Clutching the goddess's pearl to her heart, Merys stumbles to the spiral stairwell hewn directly into the mountain. Gathering her tattered skirts in her free hand, she climbs. And climbs. And climbs. The stairwell never branches. The stairs are perfectly precise and even, but slippery. Wind howls from above, whipping her hair into her eyes and against her cheeks. Her legs tremble by the time she reaches the landing, a small room that opens to the elements. Rain slicks the floor by the window that reaches from the floor to the low ceiling. Treading carefully, Merys edges to the opening and stares at the abrupt drop to the roiling ocean over two hundred feet below.

Trapped. She's trapped.

The foreign footsteps have nearly reached the tiny room. Merys squeezes the pearl and scrunches her eyes shut.

Please, Veydra…

"Mer."

"Reyvain!" Merys smiles so broad her cheeks hurt. Then she notices the stiff military jacket, black with silver buttons instead of blue with gold. How her favorite brother's eyes seem dead rather than deep. "What are you doing here?"

Her brother draws closer, eyes searching hers. "I'm here to take you home."

"Home?" Merys echoes. She reaches out, fingertips brushing one of the silver buttons glistening on his jacket. Her gaze meets his, searching for warmth and finding only cold. She swallows, but her throat feels like she's swallowed sand. "Whose home?"

A rueful smile cracks Reyvain's lips, and he settles his hands on her shoulders. "Your new home. In Gravehold."

"I don't believe this—you're my brother!" Merys flinches away. The wind whips her skirts around her ankles, reminding her how close she is to falling.

"I am." Reyvain shrugs. "I'm also the youngest of nine sons in a queendom. I'm no one and nothing. I have to fight for every little thing I want. And I *don't* want to be a footnote in history."

"I don't understand. What are you fighting for now? What do you want?"

"My own kingdom."

Merys frowns, shaking her head. "Your own… what have you done, brother?"

"Nothing Mother wouldn't have done in my position." Reyvain crosses his arms, sneering. "Did you know, when I was studying in Regalia, Ferryn Scarforger captured me? No one even noticed. Now, while the ninth son in a queendom makes a terrible bargaining chip, he can make a decent informant. In exchange for our army's movements and you, dearest sister, Ferryn has granted me the throne of Kaleirusia."

"That's impossible," Merys whispers. "Father's capture, Scarforger's ransom…it was all you?"

A cruel grin slashes across Reyvain's mouth. "You didn't leave me much choice—too timid to put that dreadful Captain Galehaven in his place or even give Mother her final rites, I knew you'd never speak up for me to have a seat on the Council."

"I—I—"

"Is that what this reckless voyage has been about, Mer? Proving something to yourself? Sailing across the sea to this remote island alone, just like mother did at our age? Well, do you feel brave now, little sister? Have you found what you're looking for?"

Merys blinks away tears. It wasn't bravery that brought her on this journey. Deep down, she knows that. She could say it was her intention to wish for her mother's life on Veydra's eye the entire time, but that would be a lie.

She didn't set out to save Kaleirusia. She didn't even chart the voyage to start with. She commandeered a ship to run from Ferryn Scarforger. From her mother's throne and crown. It was never about the destination—it was always about the escape.

Wind yanks at her hair about her face and hisses in her ears. It almost feels like fingertips prodding her ribs, pushing her toward the edge overlooking the sea. She clutches Veydra's Eye to her stomach and glances over her shoulder. Waves pummel against rocks, singing a rumbling chorus below.

"I wonder… will the king of Gravehold uphold his word if you return to him empty-handed?"

Reyvain's smug expression disintegrates. "Step away from that ledge, Merys."

Merys slides her foot backward, feeling nothing but air beneath her heel. "I hope Scarforger does to you what he did to Father when you fail to bring him his bride."

"No!" Reyvain lunges for her, but his hand closes on empty air. Merys closes her eyes.

Falling is strange. Weightless. The loud rush of air on ears, drowning out pounding blood and heartbeats. Hungry, hollowing the stomach from the inside out. Cold.

Sunlight explodes in Merys's hands. Veydra's Eye—it blazes with light and heat. The Fall presses in, the heat and pressure crushing her into a glittering diamond.

Her feet slam into solid ground, and her knees buckle. She blinks at the white marble floor, confused. She stands, slowly, and turns, taking in the cathedral ceilings and walls on either side. The wind screams behind her. There is nothing outside—a sheer drop, like this room is suspended in air. No way to go but forward. Merys turns, fingers aching from how tightly she clutches Veydra's Eye.

Strange women line the walls. Mermaids with black orca tails brace themselves on heavy spears. Some have bodies that blend into serpents. Others stand on two legs like Merys, but they could never be confused with humans. Their skin tones vary in shades of seafoam. The only indications that they're alive and not flawless marble statues are the flutter of their gills and the occasional blink.

They make no move to stop her as she shuffles down the room's center. Almost like they're standing at attention flanking an aisle, like the guards in her parents' throne room.

Merys stops and glances at the end of the room opposite the gaping hole into the sky.

A gilded throne looms on a dais, hewn from marble and crystal. An ice sculpture carved into the shape of a person sits on the cold granite. They seem to sit up straighter as Merys inches closer, a trick of the light or fatigue.

Merys stands before the ice sculpture, breath misting in the air. The figure's opaque slate-gray form blooms with color. A woman, beautiful as she is severe. Her features shift into another woman's—familiar but unknown. With a gasp, Merys recalls the portrait of Queen Asha in the library. Her many times great-ancestor fades into another woman. And another. And another, before finally settling.

She's striking, with seaweed hair that undulates in a nonexistent tide. One eye is the glassy gold of a fisheye, the other is absent from its empty socket.

Fatigue and awe buckle Merys's knees. She sinks to the floor, bracing herself on one bloody palm while crushing Veydra's Eye to her chest. "Sea Mother."

Veydra's smile reveals jagged shark teeth, but awe overwhelms the fear battering Merys's heart.

"Rise, Shore Daughter. Come closer. All Kaleirusian Queens have made the voyage to wish upon my eye. You face a choice: you may wish for happiness but shorten your life. Or a voice of strength and power, but every step will be agony."

"All queens?" Merys whispers. "Even my mother?"

Veydra nods gravely.

"What did she wish for?" Merys sighs. Her eyes still ache from the funeral, the day everything changed. "I suppose she wished for happiness—her ailment always seemed supernatural to me."

The warrior goddess's skin shifts from seafoam to a rich olive complexion. Queen Avyria stares down at her, eyebrow raised. "It's time to find your voice, Daughter dearest, Daughter mine, and join our chorus. The walk is hard, but the pain can be conquered." She leans forward in her throne. "The kingdoms require reminding that Veydra's Daughters bow to no man."

Merys manages a tremulous smile, wiping her eye with a knuckle. Despite the blood and sand clinging to the goddess's eye, it shimmers with its own incandescent light.

"I wish…"

Sharing Bubbles

R.A. Krueger

Furna

Bubbles slid over her tail fin, tickling as they popped and rose toward the surface. Furna laughed and rolled over the thermal vents again. The warmth seeping from the ground felt like a loved one's embrace, gentle and familiar. She turned onto her back, staring up through the water, watching as the pockets of air rushed away toward the distant surface. Her fins danced through the bubbles, and she closed her eyes for a brief moment.

"We better get moving or we'll be late." Furna sighed. "Again."

She pulled out the pearl she kept tucked in one of the many folds and flutters of a small side fin, and set it on her chest, the steady weight of it a constant comfort.

"You know Mother won't be happy if we miss the welcome greeting again."

She'd been tasked with the pearl's protection when she'd been just a young guppy, but she still wondered at its depth and beauty. It was larger than pearls found inside shells, which let her see the green sparks moving across its milky white surface. She held it up and marveled at the specks that spun around its glowing center, whirling around it like the many legs of an octopus.

"I've said it a thousand times, and I'll say it again," her tail flicked, and they jetted off through the water, over the rocky bottom, "you are the loveliest pearl I've ever seen."

It shimmered, almost in response to her praise. Furna smiled and tucked it away. With her fins free, she torpedoed through the water and hollered quick greetings as fish darted from her path.

Furna stopped at the edge of the seagrass forest, the long tendrils swirled up above her reaching for the surface as the bubbles had. She often wondered why everything seemed to yearn for the surface when life down here was perfectly wonderful. She slid in between the long, smooth leaves, running her fins through them as she passed.

On the other side of the forest, Furna dipped down and followed a well-worn path, the rocks and sand flattened by many tails and fins passing overhead. The vibrations in the water told her the crowd had already gathered and that she would, in fact, be late. Again.

Rounding a cliff's edge, Furna smiled. Everyone was there, gathered in a circle as they were every morning. She slid past her sister, her dark fins resting gracefully on the sand, past her brother with his tail the color of the heat seeping through the thermal vents, and she settled next to their mother.

Furna tucked her own green tail beneath her and pulled out her pearl to rest it in her lap. She ignored her mother's gentle jab and focused on her pearl. Its beautiful swirls matched her tail and were the reason she'd been given this specific pearl when it had been her time.

Her father held up his pearl, a dark, swirling, sphere speckled with pure white light at its center. He started a low hum, the vibrations like gentle waves lapping at her skin. Soon, her mother joined in, raising her golden pearl, her higher-pitched vibrations hitting Furna like the incessant seagrasses on a stormy day.

Furna added her own voice next, the perfect combination of her parents. As the rest of her family joined them, each raising their own pearl, their vibrations warbled in her ears until the final voice of her littlest sister, soft and sweet, joined theirs, and all the vibrations fell together in perfect harmony.

Their pearls were all raised high, their sound passing through and surrounding them. Filling them with their vibration's energy. The pearls shimmered and crackled in their palms. Reds. Whites. Greens. A full array of color and life. Furna closed her eyes and let the vibrations flow through her as well. Her flippers and fins flowed softly in the gentle current.

Her father's vibrations ended first, bringing the slight warble back to their hum. Without them all, their song was incomplete. Her mother's sharp vibrations ended next. Then her own.

Furna pulled her pearl back to her chest, its warmth slowly cooling as water passed around it.

"Come tomorrow's light. Keep them safe. Keep them well," her father bowed his head.

"Keep them safe. Keep them well," everyone repeated.

Criton

Criton's suit was stiff from not being stored properly after his last water dive. He knew his latest hire was worthless. Well, not worthless. There was plenty of poop to be scooped in all the pens on the ship. And Criton would make sure that's exactly where that young man ended up after this exploration.

"Approaching a tenth of a klick, sir," his assistant's voice sounded in his ear.

Criton turned his head to the rest of his team. Only four of them were able to dive to such depths. He could handle going down further, but some of his crew came from much more fragile species with thinner skeletal structures. His mind briefly drifted to computing the effect lighter planetary gravity had on the bones of the inhabitants, something he'd studied at length several years ago. The skeletons were still on display on his ship. Removing the flesh had been equally as educational, but he'd been rather single-minded in his research then.

"This is deep enough. We can see the bottom from here," he spoke into the microphone. "No lights. Stay in pairs. Keep within a tenth of a klick of this location."

They each reached out and tapped a button on their suits. In the semi-darkness, they couldn't see the tethers shoot out but could feel them tugging slightly as the water moved around them. As they typed a tenth of a klick into their tether monitors, he typed a quarter klick into his own and turned away from them.

"I expect three unique samples from each of you," he said without turning back. "Alive, if possible, but we can still learn a lot if they're dead."

"Yes, Sir."

Criton swam down further, closer to the bottom. He blinked his inner eyelid, forcing his pupils to dilate and allow in more light. Soon, he was able to see as easily as if he were on the surface at dusk. It wasn't ideal, but far better than scaring off possible samples with a headlamp.

A grouping of seagrasses rose in front of him, rising almost the full quarter klick above him. He examined their leaves for a moment, quickly realizing nothing was unique about them, and pushed through briskly. When he came through on the opposite side, he could feel the pull of his tether monitor telling him he was close to his limit.

Criton sighed but said nothing due to the microphone in his helmet. He could hear his team quietly chattering in the background and he didn't want to add his voice to the distracting noise. He was about to turn back when he noticed a worn path along the seafloor beneath him.

Ah ha.

Criton adjusted the distance on his tether monitor, removing the limitation altogether, and swam slowly along the trail below him. As he rounded a rock wall, a vibration through the water hit him like a hungry Galactadon.

Criton picked himself up from the sea floor and adjusted his helmet. Cautiously, he looked around the edge of the rocks. At first, all he saw was a mass of vibrating frills. But soon he was able to distinguish individual bodies.

Their faces were slightly humanoid, similar to the land creatures here on Earth, but covered in small scales instead of skin. On their heads were, what Criton guessed to be, multiple antennas, but had the appearance of the seagrasses he'd just swum through. Easy camouflage, no doubt. Their lean tails were almost completely hidden by layers of long, flowing fins from their sides. There must have been seven or eight of them.

Some kind of mating ritual probably.

Criton had never seen anything like them. On all the planets he'd studied. Of all the creatures he'd captured. Whatever these were, they captivated him. He couldn't take his eyes off them as they vibrated and keened in a mass of fluttering fins.

He pressed the button on his tether monitor to bring his team to his location.

"I found a large sample. Be silent. Be prepared," he said through the mic.

"Yes, Sir." He could hear the water rushing past their helmets as they hurried in his direction, yanked from whatever they were doing by their tether system.

They needed to hurry. Whatever was happening with his samples was ending, and he didn't want to lose them. He wanted one to study.

He needed one.

Furna

Furna's family slowly drifted away, but she was in no rush. She had listened to her sister talk about teaching the guppies and her mom complain about the seaweed popping up around the carefully culti-vated coral in her garden. These moments filled her heart every day. She spun, her fins fanning out in a wide circle, and smiled. It was going to be a great day; she could feel it.

She darted off toward the forest, ready to hunt for some food. Tuck-ing her fins in, she slipped through the tall sea grass, barely grazing the ground. A cluster of shells at the base of a large rock caught her eye, and she stopped to crack them open and slurp out the goopy insides. They slid down her throat as she started hunting for more. One of her favorite spots, just outside the forest, was usually full of large shells. She scoured the ground, running her fins through the sandy patches between pitted rocks. Her search slowed as a large shadow fell over her.

Furna glanced up, expecting a playful dolphin or curious shark. She reeled back at the sight of an unknown shape above her, scraping her fin against the hard stone. The creature floated close to her, staring at her through large, dark eyes. It wore a suit like the few humans she'd seen, but this was different. Shimmery instead of dark, it didn't seem to hinder its movements as the creature floated there calmly.

It tilted its head at her, obviously curious, too. Furna's eyes darted around, sensing for any danger. But all she saw was the forest at her back and open waters before them. The creature lowered itself to the ground, balancing on two stiff fin-like appendages. Furna, forgetting any caution, darted forward to study the creature, marveling at its balancing skills. She surged around its lower fins, realizing they weren't like fins at all. More like humans but bent oddly. Furna spun around it, fins gliding over its smooth suit, inspecting its body all the way up to its head. She pressed an eye to the hard, clear covering over its face. She'd hoped to share bubbles, but that wouldn't be possible if it were completely enclosed.

The creature bared its teeth, making a loud, sharp sound. Furna jumped back, clasping her fins to her chest. Its whole body shook as it continued to make the noise. After a moment of fear, Furna realized it was a happy sound. The creature was happy to see her. Furna had traveled the whole ocean, meeting all types of creatures. She knew that until she could share bubbles with them, the best way to put a strange creature at ease was to mimic its behavior. So, Furna bared her teeth and made a similar bark-wheeze sound at the creature, which made it shake even more.

It continued to make sounds at her, flapping its upper fin-like limbs around. Furna held out a fin, curious if it would allow her to touch it. She held it between them, not wanting to frighten it. The creature stilled and watched her face, then her fin. Slowly, it raised its side fin to reach out to her. It's side fin was hard and large, nothing like her soft, flowy one.

Furna cocked her head to the side, curious about where this creature had come from. No humans ever made it to the ground here, and this creature obviously wasn't human. So, what was it and how did it get here?

She glanced up, looking for where it might have come from, and caught a glimpse of movement just behind them. Her eyes flew back to the creature's face. It glanced behind her. Furna whirled around, fins fanning out around her body in defense.

Three more creatures in shimmery suits shot out of the forest. Furna threw her fins out even wider, making herself as large as possible, but it was nowhere near large enough. Each creature was at least double her size. Why did she let her curiosity get the best of her? Didn't her mother always say it'd get her in trouble?

Furna let out a shrieking hum, the highest pitch reserved only for danger. The vibrations shook the seagrass behind the creatures as they closed in on her. She spun slowly in a circle as they surrounded her. She shrieked again, hoping her family would burst through the forest while also hoping they were as far away from this danger as possible.

She shrieked a third time and planned to hold it for as long as possible. The four creatures stopped moving, and she turned back to the first one. His eyes held hers for a moment before they dropped to the ground. It pushed at something on its side fin and silvery threads shot out around her. Everywhere they touched, they burned for an instant then her fins fell numb to her side. Fluttering uselessly, unfeeling, and wrapped in shiny threads. Once her fins had fallen, the threads landed on her head, and after a quick jolt, her shrieking finally stopped. Paralyzed.

Furna could barely breathe, not because the silver threads froze her lungs, but from fear. The creatures dragged her towards the surface. Her eyes darted around, desperate. The first creature would no longer look at her and passed off the threads holding her to one of the other creatures. They ascended quickly, the water becoming too warm and far too bright. Furna flopped along behind them, her body useless but her mind still alert. She rolled upside down as they tugged her along, watching as the ground disappeared in the distance.

Finally, she felt a responding vibration. She heard their shrieks as these creatures pulled her from the water. Her family had come. But it was too late.

Criton

His diving suit was being cleaned and stored by a veteran crew member, while the latest hire was shoveling his first of many, many buckets of poop. Criton sighed. Nothing annoyed him more than incompetence.

The main hall of his ship gleamed as he slowly walked towards the quarantine bay. It was lined with windows, each looking into an immaculate enclosure. He'd found and brought back to his ship creatures from all over the galaxy. Every size, shape, and color imaginable. From every kind of environment imaginable.

He'd found an amphibious Fallowmxx on an acid planet. A ten-legged Shirtel twenty times his size. A Rhinot currently living under a microscope because it was a fully functioning organism barely larger than an atom.

He'd built this ship from nothing, determined to have the leading research lab in the galaxy with the largest display of species available. It was his pride and joy. His life's greatest achievement.

Then, why, for the first time ever, did he not feel a surge of accomplishment as he peered into the enclosures he passed?

I laughed.

That was why. When was the last time he'd laughed? It had sputtered out of him, like the gurgle of a dying Goartmas. A rusty sound he hadn't even recognized.

This new sample he had yet to name. It had been so curious, so trusting, that it'd been comical. When it pressed its face up to his helmet, he'd lost it. Only for a few moments, but it had affected him. It still was.

He hadn't even been able to meet the creature's eyes as he shot the net over it. He always watched to see how a new sample reacted to the electrical impulse. It was an important detail to include in the case study.

Criton squared his shoulders. It was bad enough that his team heard his laughter over the mic, and that he'd missed crucial data for the report. He would not allow some misguided emotional attachment to a sample derail his work.

He pushed through the quarantine bay doors and approached the water tank where the new sample would be kept until a permanent enclosure could be created to fit its specific requirements. The creature lay unmoving at the bottom and dread jolted through his system. He could still glean valuable information from a corpse, but he'd really hoped to study this one alive first.

Then it stirred, a slight movement of a fin. But it was enough. Criton unclenched his jaw and turned to the quarantine techs.

"Let's get to work. We have multiple new samples to catalog." He snapped at the crew milling around the water tank.

The creature was beautiful, so he didn't blame them for being overly curious. But inefficiency was not to be tolerated. They scampered to the other tanks and cages in the room, but their eyes kept darting back to the water tank.

This creature was captivating, like the mermaids or sirens from Earth's mythology. When the creature lifted its head, its eyes locked onto Criton's. He knew he saw pain there. Maybe the electrical charges from the net were more debilitating for these creatures since they lived in water. That was a theory he would normally test out, but the thought of doing that to this sample turned his stomachs sour.

"This one is mine. I am the only one to run tests on this sample. Understood?"

"Yes, Sir."

Furna

She pressed herself to the bottom of the clear container she was in, refusing to move. Her eyes darted around and her heart beat wildly. Where was she? What were they going to do to her?

All around her were crates and cages full of creatures, some she recognized and some she didn't. The air was filled with their sounds. Moaning, calling for loved ones, pain. It was the sound of misery. She could feel each vibration against her skin, sharp and cutting like the edge of a shark's tooth. Her tail still tingled from those threads. She could move it again, but it stung when she tried. So, she didn't try.

Furna patted her small side fin that held her pearl. She let out a deep breath when she felt that it was still there. In all that had happened, she'd forgotten to keep it safe. Instead, she'd been too focused on keeping herself safe. Her father would be so disappointed. But, Furna realized, he would probably never know. Her chest tightened as her fin clutched the pearl even harder.

And then she saw it.

The creature who'd tricked her. Who'd made happy sounds with her. Then shot her with shocking threads and dragged her away from her family. From her home. They'd connected. She'd mimicked its sounds, and they'd liked it. But it had all been a trick. A distraction.

She met its eyes. And she saw pain there. It was quickly replaced with curiosity, but she knew what she saw.

The creature had changed from its shimmery water suit and now wore a dark, scratchy-looking one. And it no longer had the clear cover over its face. Furna thought it wasn't that different from her own. Two eyes, ears. It had a flat nose, basically just two slits. And it didn't have shimmering scales like she did; its face was completely smooth. Almost pure white. Like her pearl without the beautiful green swirls and sparks.

Bright lights flashed overhead, and loud noises shook her water. Her eyes moved from one creature to another, the ones who weren't in cages. They all wore white scratchy-looking suits, except the one in front of her. They stepped away from the cages and spread out their bottom fins. Furna crept up off the bottom slightly to get a better look, but the flashing lights were so bright it hurt to keep her eyes open.

The water cage she was in began to shake. They all began to shake. Furna pressed herself to the bottom again and squeezed her eyes shut. Shaking ground was never a good thing. A dangerous thermal vent. A cascade of dropping rocks. She held her breath, waiting for something to happen. But all she felt was the sensation of lifting up, and then nothing. The lights and loud noise stopped. Her water stopped shaking. The white-suited creatures started moving again.

The dark-suited creature had placed its fin against her container to steady himself while the ground shook. Furna darted off the bottom. Her tail stung. Her fins felt stiff, but she knew this was her chance. She had to make a connection. If she could share bubbles, they could figure this out. She just knew it.

Furna pressed her fin against theirs, the cold hard container the only thing between them. They'd done this before. In her home. It had to remind the creature of that. She moved to be eye level with it, which pushed her head to the surface of her tiny container. She could feel the uncomfortable dryness as her antenna left the water. She needed them closer.

She raised her head up, more and more of her face leaving the water. Her eyes squeezed shut, tight against the dry air. The creature leaned in, its curiosity peaked. Outside the water, her face began to tingle. The wetness on her scales was drying up too fast, and if she stayed there too long, they would dull and die. She needed the creature to get a little closer. She forced her eyes open, ignoring the burning, and looked deep into its gaze.

It leaned forward slightly, probably unconsciously, but it was enough. With a splash, Furna pushed off from the bottom of her container, wrapped her fins around its surprised face, and dragged it back down with her. She pressed its face to one of her ears, then the other. She rushed to press her mouth to both of its ears too. The creature was screaming and losing all its bubbles quickly. Furna twisted its head to get the last of its bubbles and pressed her mouth to theirs. She inhaled the last of the bubbles from its mouth. She pulled back for only a moment but looked at the shocked expression on the creature's face. Then pressed her mouth to its again, forcing her own air into its lungs just as the white-suited creatures dragged the dark one from her grasp.

She hoped it had been enough. They'd know soon.

Criton

He ended up in a soaking wet jumble on the floor with two of his crew. He ripped his arms from their grasp and surged to his feet. His breathing came in fast, heavy pants.

"Are you okay, sir?" One of the crew clasped onto his arm again, no doubt in an attempt to steady him, but it just angered him further.

"He's fine."

Criton whirled around to the female crew member several cages over. He stalked towards her, watching her face shift from shock to terror. He towered over her, dripping onto her record book.

"What did you say?" He growled. "I will not tolerate insolence aboard my ship."

"I- I- I didn't..." she was crouching now as he leaned closer to her.

"You didn't what?" he asked.

"She didn't say anything."

"Who's saying that?" he demanded.

Criton spun back around to the crew who'd helped him. Both male. Obviously not the feminine voice he was hearing. Did oxygen deprivation affect him that quickly? How long had he been under the water?

"I am."

Criton's eyes left the two confused crew members and darted around the quarantine bay.

"Over here. Yep. There you go. Right here."

Criton's eyes settled on the creature's water tank. It was staring right at him.

"Hello. I'm Furna," the creature tilted her head at him in greeting.

"This isn't... How can I?..." Criton stammered.

"Sir, are you all right?" One of the male crew members stepped forward. "Should we get medical?"

"Step aside." He rushed back to the side of the tank, shoving the two crew back onto the soaked floor. "What did you do to me?"

"We shared bubbles," the creature shrugged its shoulders as if that made complete sense.

"Shared bubbles? What does that even mean?" Criton ran a hand through his wet hair. "This shouldn't be possible."

"Possible or not, here we are."

Criton stared at the creature, ignoring the fluttering of his crew members at his back. He was racking his brain to come up with a logical explanation for what was happening but was coming up with nothing. So, he decided he was having a stress-induced mental snap, which wasn't too far-fetched; he'd been feeling emotionally off all day. Either that, or he'd just made the greatest scientific finding of his career.

Pursing his lips, he held up a finger to the creature. He took several steps towards the door before realizing it wouldn't know what that meant since it didn't have fingers.

"One moment, please."

Please? He'd just asked a glorified fish for a moment. Politely.

Criton rushed towards the door, leaving a trail of water for the crew to clean up. He headed straight for his quarters. He definitely needed a moment.

Furna

She waited for the creature to come back. It hadn't shared its name, just rushed away leaving the rest of the white-suited creatures scurrying around the room. That creature, the one who tricked her, was obviously a leader of some sort. Its dark suit set it apart, but she could also tell by the way the others responded to it. Feared it.

Now they feared her too. They stayed far away from her clear container. They washed and scrubbed the floor everywhere else, but none of them would come near her. She wasn't interested in sharing bubbles with them though.

Furna waited until the rest of the white-suited creatures left. She waited until the bright lights clicked off. And still, the dark creature did not return. Furna swam round and round the tiny container, agitation and fear mixing in her mind. What if it never came back? What if it didn't come back before they did something horrible to her? Were they going to eat her? Tear her into tiny pieces? Possibility after possibility rolled through her mind, each one worse than the one before.

Then the worst possibility of all flooded her mind, dark as squid ink. Furna sank to the bottom of her container and pulled out her pearl. It was her duty to protect it. And again, she'd been selfishly thinking of herself.

She stared into its depths. The sparks— stars and planets she'd dreamed of since she was little. The swirls— a galaxy. How many thousands of times had she thought about what life in those tiny sparkles must be like? Her one life meant nothing compared to losing the pearl.

As she stared at it, one sparkle flickered and then disappeared. Furna blinked staring at the spot it had been, needing it to reappear. But that space was dark. Her chest felt tight as she curled around the pearl at the bottom of her container. She should have dropped the pearl to her family before being pulled from the water. If she hadn't been thinking only about herself, if she hadn't been so selfish, that sparkle would still exist. She curled even tighter around it, squeezing her eyes shut to keep out the foreign world around her.

The bright lights above flickered back to life. Furna blinked, her eyes feeling like she'd rolled in sand. The pearl lay heavy on her chest. More darkness had spread through its outer border. Furna knew it needed their first light ritual. Needed their vibrations and energy. She hoped hers alone would be enough to keep it going until... Until when?

Until she got it back home. She wasn't going to lose hope so soon.

She raised the pearl above her and began to hum. Her vibrations were weak compared to what her whole family could provide their pearls. But she'd do everything she could.

She closed her eyes and hummed with all her strength. The vibrations bounced off the sides of the tiny container, making them erratic and ineffective. Furna tried all different angles in the tiny space until she found a way to use the sides to amplify and direct her vibrations. Then, she went through the whole ritual for the first time on her own.

It hurt her heart, but also made her feel closer to them. She knew they were doing the same thing right now. Trying to figure out how to fix the warble in their vibrations without her.

When she hummed the last note, she sighed. It wouldn't be enough. But it was all she could do.

"So that's not a mating ritual then."

Furna spun to see the dark creature standing beside her container, far enough away to be out of her reach. It looked like it was trying to hide its agitation and unease by forcing itself to relax, its limbs hanging rigidly at its sides.

"Mating? No." She shook her head in confusion. "The humming is to share our energy. Mating is to share our bodies."

"Share your energy?" He stepped closer, his curiosity winning against his weariness. "With whom?"

"So, you're comfortable talking to me now?" Furna sidestepped the question.

"Comfortable? No." The creature tilted its head. "Curious, yes."

"I suppose curiosity will have to do." She moved to the edge of her container, getting as close to it as possible. "For now."

"Your intellect is quite surprising. And astounding."

"As is yours."

The creature made that sharp, happy sound again, and Furna relaxed slightly.

"Now, shall we try this again?" She raised her fin and placed it against the clear wall in front of her. "My name is Furna."

"My name is Captain Criton of the A.R.C." The creature straightened itself to its full height, pulling its upper fins back. "I am commander of this vessel, but a research scientist above all else."

"Captain." Furna nodded at him. "I would like to discuss my immediate release."

Criton

"We're already lightyears from your home planet, Furna." Criton pursed his lips. "So, your immediate release is not possible."

"Lightyears away?" Furna asked quietly.

"Yes. My ship travels across the galaxy to study new species and acquire samples for continued research and observation."

Criton watched her face, wondering what kind of expression she'd have at this news. Confusion? Sorrow? Anger? He was shocked again when he saw none of those things. In her tightened jaw and squared shoulders, Criton saw determination. Grit, as his mother would have called it.

"So, you steal creatures from their homes, rip them from their families, place them in tiny containers, and expect accurate data for your research?"

Criton cringed at the steely tone of her voice as well as the truth of her words. This is something his critics had brought up in the past, and he'd always been able to brush it off with quick reassurances that they did everything to replicate their homes down to the smallest details. But hearing it from one of the samples themselves, especially from her, was like a sliver to his heart, the kind that keeps burrowing deeper until it festers and eventually bursts.

He opened his mouth to tell her the same things he told his critics, but the words that usually flowed so easily wouldn't come. So, he closed his mouth and said nothing.

"You know I'm right."

It wasn't a question.

Criton watched as something passed through Furna. Hesitation, possibly. She turned from him briefly and hung her head. When she faced him again, she held something in her fins.

"Criton. We don't really know each other. But for some reason that goes against everything you've shown me, I feel like I can trust you." Her eyes flicked up to meet his. "Can I trust you?"

"Yes." He didn't hesitate.

"My life has a sole purpose. My family, all of us do. A purpose I will put above all else, including my own life," Furna paused, shuddering slightly, "I will do everything in my power to protect this."

She held her fin up to him like she'd done several times before, but this time, pressed against the glass, Criton could see something circular and white.

"A pearl?" he raised an eyebrow in question.

"Look closer."

Criton knelt at the side of her tank and pressed his face as close to the pearl as he could. For a moment he saw only the milky white surface, but as he stared, green flecks appeared. Criton gasped as the glowing nucleus came into focus. He could clearly see the spiral arms and the halo.

"How?" he whispered.

"Look at the outside edge," Furna said softly.

Criton tore his gaze away from the swirling center to the outer arms. His eyes darted from star to star until he noticed one flickering. It flashed slower and slower until it disappeared into the darkness at the edge of the pearl.

"It's dying," Furna said. "I don't have the energy alone to keep it going. I need my family."

Criton tore his eyes from the pearl and looked at Furna. Really looked at her. The deep beautiful green of her tail and fins was graying at the edges. The antenna on top of her head that floated so gracefully in the waters of Earth, hung limp beside her face. Criton knew the pearl wasn't the only thing dying.

"We'll take you both back." The words fell from his mouth before the thought even formed in his brain.

"Take the rest of them back first."

"What?"

"The other creatures on this ship." Furna tucked the pearl back under one of her smaller pectoral fins. "Take them back first."

"I don't think you understand how big this ship is, Furna."

Criton grabbed the control pad for her tank and pressed a few buttons. It rose from the ground and followed him as he walked out through the quarantine bay doors. He led her slowly down the main hallway of his ship, showing her the enclosures they'd built for all the species he'd sampled.

Furna pressed her fins to the glass of her container, her face lit in a mixture of wonder and concern.

"I never knew," she finally said. "I never knew there were so many."

"I told you there'd be too many to return."

"No," She shook her head, sending small droplets of water onto Criton's sleeve. "I've stared at this pearl my whole life wondering about the lives it contains," she stopped and looked all around her, "and never once wondered about the lives here with me in my own world."

"Galaxy," Criton corrected. "These creatures all come from our galaxy. I've traveled every bit of it. Seen every planet and star there is to see."

"Show me."

"What? The entire galaxy?" Criton shook his head. "It would take too long. You don't have that kind of time."

"Return them all and show me."

Criton met her eyes, the deepest green he'd ever seen. He saw a curiosity that mirrored his own. But also saw something he was certain his eyes did not contain. Compassion. Criton sucked air in through clenched teeth as the sliver in his heart burrowed a little deeper.

She's right.

"It would be suicide, Furna."

"As long as the pearl survives, I've done my job. I know it's selfish, but I want to experience my own galaxy and marvel at all its sparkles like I've done with this pearl all my life." Furna continued to spin, staring at the vast array of creatures surrounding her.

"Aside from the obvious dangers to yourself," Criton paused, raising an eyebrow, "you're asking me to give up my life's work."

"I'm doing no such thing."

Furna stuck her fins to her side, looking like a stubborn child with their hands balled up on their hips. Criton turned his back to her, looking around, trying to take it in like she was. Seeing it with fresh eyes.

"You can still study creatures," Furna's voice softened. "Your research would be more accurate seeing them on their home planets, interacting with their own families, eating their favorite foods, being happy."

Criton looked at the nearest enclosure. A single solitary creature lay in the farthest corner, curled into a ball. He stepped to the next enclosure and saw the same thing. The sample was pressed into a small cave at the back.

"Being happy…" Criton repeated her last words to himself as he walked down the hall, seeing creature after creature alone, unmoving, and afraid. "Maybe you're right."

Maybe they've all been right.

He thought of his critics, telling him the same things Furna was telling him now. Why hadn't it sunk in all the times he'd heard it in the past? Why did it take capturing an alluring aquatic creature on Earth, of all places, for him to see the truth?

"I know I'm right." Furna floated patiently in her tank. "I can tell you right now, I'm not going to act like my normal self in this tiny tank, surrounded by creatures who don't understand me. I'm just lucky we can share bubbles."

"Lucky indeed." Criton returned to the side of her tank, pondering what she'd just told him.

Maybe it did take hearing from one of his captured samples to make it real. Maybe that's why it finally made sense. Who better to tell him his research was flawed than a creature he was researching?

"You have a point. One that I'm considering." Criton rubbed his chin while doing some calculations. "But, again, Furna, at the rate your fins have already begun to deteriorate, I can't imagine you have more than four or five weeks."

"Could you return all these creatures in that time?"

"It would be possible, but it would be an extremely tight schedule." Criton shook his head. "And my calculation could be inaccurate. They are nothing more than a preliminary estimate."

"I've never seen anything outside my own ocean." Furna pursed her lips and then nodded as if making a decision. "I've stared at the pearl my whole life wondering about it. Now that I know I could see my own galaxy, I want to see it all. I have to think I was brought here for a reason. I have to believe that."

"And what about your pearl?" Criton glanced at the sphere in her fin. "I don't have any calculations for how long it will survive."

"How about this? As long as the pearl still glows, we can return these creatures, and you show me worlds I've only dreamed of."

We. We return these creatures...

He was never part of 'we.' It was always 'I' and 'me,' but never 'we.' Even with the crew, he kept himself apart. At a young age, his father had told him that superior beings, whether that be by intelligence, status, or species, should hold themselves to a higher standard and set themselves apart, lest they lower themselves to the level of their inferiors. Criton had always prospered on his own and never felt a need to be included, even with his own peers.

Furna had done something amazing to him by sharing bubbles, so didn't see her as a lesser being, but as an equal. And something about the excitement and lack of hesitation in her voice made him want to work with her. Wanted to be a part of her 'we.' He'd never known he was missing out, working and living in such solitude. And now that he knew how it felt, the thought of losing it was unbearable.

"Ok. *We* can do that."

Furna

Over the next month, Furna saw more than she ever could have imagined. She saw worlds more different than anything she could fathom. They released creature after creature on planet after planet. Her heart and mind were constantly racing, even as her body was slowing down.

She knew it.

He knew it.

She was dying.

The longer she and her pearl were away from home, the weaker they became. Her tail, which had been beautiful shades of green, was now gray. Her fins felt like weights at her sides, but still, she marveled at the sights she was seeing.

Her pearl, which she was humming and feeding her vibrations multiple times a day now, had only a single ball of light at its center. All the beautiful sparkles and swirls had disappeared into the darkness. She was scared they'd been gone too long, that her selfishness was causing too much damage. But they were on their final stop before returning to Earth. It just needed to hold out a little while longer. They both did.

Furna turned her head slowly to look at Criton. His cheeks were rosy as he talked with his crewmates. As much as she loved seeing the planets and the creatures that lived there, the thing she'd enjoyed seeing most was Criton's slow transformation. As if, somehow, the life that was leaving her body was seeping into his.

With most of the creatures gone from the rest of the ship, the crew had started gathering in the quarantine bay. At first, the extra bodies and lack of jobs agitated Criton to the point of distraction. Now, he leaned against their workstation gesturing wildly with his hands as they mapped out the future plans for the ship.

"Don't you think so, Furna?" He looked over his shoulder, eyes instantly filling with concern.

"Sorry, what?" Furna focused on saying. Speaking had become quite taxing over the past week, so she found herself saying less and less.

"Furna, are you alright?" Criton hurried over to her carrier. The one he'd designed to allow her to fully experience all the planets. It was fully enclosed, had top-of-the-line filtration and hover engines on the bottom and sides for pristine water and easy maneuverability. Or so he'd told her. She knew nothing about those sorts of things.

"I'm fine, Criton." She settled on the bottom of the tank, resting her arms on the shelf he'd built on the side. She rested her chin on her arms and gave him a small smile. "Just thinking."

"We can skip the next stop," he whispered, "take you home first. You have my word I'll complete our mission."

"Finish the mission." She closed her eyes. "Return them all."

There were so many more words she wanted to say but couldn't find the energy. Criton placed his palm against the glass, as was their tradition now, and turned back to the crew to finish plans.

"One more adventure."

Criton

His ship raced towards Earth. It was moving faster than ever, with so little weight and cargo inside. They'd be there soon and Criton prayed it would be soon enough.

"Full speed," he told the pilot. "Don't let up for anything."

"Yes, Captain."

He left the command deck and rushed to the quarantine bay. He pulled on his dive suit as the rest of the crew hurried from one crate to the next, making sure all the creatures from Earth were secure on the transport vehicles and ready to go.

Furna lay at the bottom of her tank, barely breathing. He'd found her like that this morning. Nothing they did could entice her to even sit up. Not even the freshest oysters they could find. The pearl lay at her side, flickering against her ashen fins.

"Furna, dear, we'll be there in minutes." He sighed as her eyes cracked open. "Just hold on for me. Please."

He hurried to attach his seat to the control desk on her tank. He could monitor everything from here. Stay by her side the whole time.

"Criton?" Her tiny voice called to him, whisper-thin. "The pearl?"

"Still flickering. Don't worry. It will be fine."

She smiled slightly as he stared at the pearl. Its surface had turned from milky white to black. Only a small pin-rick of light flickered at its center. Over the past few days, the time between flickers became longer and longer. Neither Furna nor Criton mentioned it, but they knew. Time was slim for them both.

Criton maneuvered Furna's tank to the front of the transport line. Behind him were large and small crates full of the magnificent creatures of Earth. A massive pachyderm. An eight-legged insect that spun silk webbing from its abdomen. A canine obsessed with a small yellow ball. Earth had, by far, the vastest array of life forms. Yet one species was terminating the rest through neglect, apathy, and cruelty. Criton shook his head, hoping the specimens they'd studied would survive on such a hostile planet. He'd argued with Furna, to no avail, about the possibility of these species going extinct without his intervention.

He'd known she was right. All this time he'd known. It took a breathtaking aquatic species from Earth to make him admit it. Damn his pride and lust for knowledge.

"Furna," he tapped into their own private mic system, "since you'll be leaving in a few minutes, I wanted to say thank you. For showing me a better way. For standing up to me when no one else would. For sharing your bubbles with me."

The corners of her mouth turned up, but otherwise, she didn't respond. She didn't need to. She'd already thanked him a hundred times for their 'adventures,' as she called them. Seeing their galaxy together, through her eyes, was like seeing it for the first time.

The overhead lights dimmed, letting them know they'd begun their descent. Only minutes now.

"Almost there, Furna. We're so close," he whispered. "Soon you'll be back in your saline waters and kelp forests."

No response this time.

Criton checked the monitors. Heartbeat and respirations were decreasing.

The ship landed with a soft thump.

"Get that door open," he yelled at the crew manning the cargo door. "Now!"

They overrode the pully release mechanism, and the door crashed down. Criton rushed out through the blinding light. He drove the tank over sand and into the welcoming waves. He stopped just as the tank was submerged.

"We're here, my dear. We made it."

Criton rushed to the top of the tank, tearing at the latches to open the door. He dove inside and grabbed Furna from the bottom as fresh seawater rushed in.

She felt so insubstantial, like nothing more than draping his lab coat over his arms. He surfaced in the tank. He jumped out, sheltering her as they moved through the air, and landed in the ocean water. He sank down under the waves and cradled her in his lap.

"Do you feel it, Furna?" He asked through the mic in his helmet. "You're home."

Her eyes finally opened. That deep, beautiful green in a stark white face.

"Thank…" she whispered over cracked lips, "…you."

She raised her fin to his face, and he leaned into her touch. Furna sighed as the waves gently rocked them together. Back and forth. Her hand slowly slid from his face and her eyes drifted closed.

Criton watched as the pearl slipped from her grasp. It drifted down and rolled out to deeper waters, black against the white sand.

The current carried the black pearl out, deeper and deeper. It rolled off the edge of a rock face, down into a ravine. Down into waiting fins. Rushed through the seagrass forest. Down the path. Held high as vibrations filled it with energy. Filled it with love and song. The vibrations continued until, at last, a pinprick of green light exploded from its center. The light didn't flicker but held strong.

Then it was passed into a pair of tiny, new fins. Full of energy and life.

Descent

Chelsea M. Brown

A leftover tradition from when she was younger, Delta Rivera woke early on Sunday and headed to the beach.

The sun crept up the sky as she walked across the gritty sand. The smell of the sea was always stronger the days after a storm. While scanning the waterfront, she fingered a coin hanging on a delicate chain around her neck.

It was worth a pretty penny, she assumed. The silver was stamped with the worn face of Isabel II, the former Queen of Spain and the Philippines, on one side and a royal crest on the flipside. Finding a piece of history inspired her to keep searching, to look beneath the surface, to uncover what else was lost to time.

It became an obsession, one she nurtured, long after her abuelito and younger brother lost interest in going with her. When she was ten, Lito used to wake her—then Dylan, a few years later—and take them to Carrigan Beach. They went every weekend and after heavy storms if the kids were on school breaks. He'd bought a MetalLab metal detector when he retired and took them along the beach to search for lost items or treasures that washed onto shore. They went out together dutifully for two years before they'd given up, and she'd been going alone now every weekend for the past five years.

Her first discovery felt like she'd won the lottery. She got that same feeling of accomplishment and glory every time she dug something from the ground. More often than not, there was nothing, but occasionally, she dug up a trinket, like a broken necklace or worn ring. One time, and this was the most excited she'd ever been when treasure hunting, she discovered the coin on her necklace.

The MetalLab vibrated in her hand, and her heart ping-ponged in her chest. As she got closer, the detector called out, singing to her that there was an object below the surface. She swung the detector slowly around the area to learn the extent of the object's dimensions, lowered it to the ground, once she established its boundaries, and pulled the spade from her backpack.

Hope sprang up in her chest. What could it be, she wondered, as she dug. She wanted another coin, something to tell her she was on the right path to something bigger. When her spade touched metal, she switched to digging with her fingers. Her hope hit a crescendo until it burst around her and fell back to the sea with the tide. A damaged pair of glasses lay in the sand.

With an outraged groan, she tossed them into her pack, picked up the MetalLab, and got back to walking the beach. She knew better than to raise her expectations like that. She found junk frequently, but there were those few times when she found something worthwhile.

When she found a dangly earring, with chipped coating over the metal, she almost gave up for the day. She was scheduled to work later that day and wanted to shower and rest before entertaining kids for the entire afternoon.

But she couldn't leave. Hope had taken root in her chest and blossomed for the day. She had a gut feeling and had to see it through.

As the sun beat down on her and the sweat rolled down her face, she cursed but didn't give up. Not yet. She knew there was something out there. There had to be. She felt it. The urge to keep going formed a pit in her chest, tugging her further.

It had stormed during the week, causing the tide to bring the sea floor to shore. If she was going to find anything in the sand, today was the day. Almost every time she'd found something valuable, it had been within days of a storm. Hurricanes were best for the search—they disrupted the area more than any other storm—but they were unreliable. She couldn't count on when they would occur, and even when they happened, they veered around too much, sometimes jumping the coast of northeast Florida entirely.

She was about to give up, to get her compulsion under control for the day, when the detector vibrated again. Moving it a little further along the beach caused it to beep. The further she moved, the louder the sound grew.

A small squeak slipped from her lips. With a hesitant step forward, the detector beeped again, louder and stronger. She found the boundary of the object and, with a bated breath, knelt on the hot, unforgiving sand.

Finally, her fingers hit something. When it didn't feel like metal, she shifted the direction of her digging, but she encountered the same material there, too. She decided to dig it out and get it out of her way. She got her fingers around the small bead-like objects and pulled gently. A chain of pearls came loose from the hardened sand, one pearl at a time until she held a gold and pearl rosary. Her thumb brushed over the dangling end and cleared the grime away to reveal it wasn't a rosary. It had a charm, carved with what appeared to be a saint's medal surrounded by tiny diamonds. Even dirty, it was the most beautiful thing she'd ever seen.

As she tucked it safely into her backpack and turned toward home, her compulsions quieted. Dr. Fromm had warned her not to give into compulsions, but how could she listen when they led to discoveries like this one?

In a daze, Delta wandered into her house. She had left the Metal-Lab in the garage and carried the chain daintily in her hands, staring at it with such pride. She felt this way when she found something. A sense of accomplishment overcame her.

"Morning, mi cariña."

Shocked out of her daze, she stumbled into a kitchen stool. In the breakfast nook off the kitchen, Abuelita sat with the newspaper and an espresso cup on the table in front of him. He smirked when he rattled her.

"Anything good today?" He tucked the paper over itself and laid it on the table, his eyebrow piqued.

Fighting the urge to hide the chain in her pocket, she nodded and held it up. He wouldn't steal it from her, even if it was worth something, but she still felt protective over it.

"Looks like a find. I'd love to see it after you clean it up. You headed to research it now?"

"Yeah, until I have to work."

"You scheduled at the pool or the Clam?"

"Clam."

"Bueno. It does you no good to sit in a chair all day. You belong to the water."

He picked his paper up, and she took the dismissal as it was intended and headed to her room.

Delta stopped by the bathroom to clean the chain and ducked into her bedroom. She laid the treasure on her desk and measured it. From end to end of the necklace loop, it measured approximately 24 inches. A 6-inch pendant hung from the center of the chain, which alternated between gold loops and round white pearls. The pendant, which she had mistakenly assumed was of a saint, had the relief of a noble young woman. A phrase curved around her head.

Viva la Reina Infantil

The phrase tickled her mind. She recognized it but couldn't recall from when or where. It felt like déjà vu, a hazy memory she couldn't quite grasp.

She pulled out her laptop and searched for a translation for the phrase, rubbing the coin charm around her neck for luck.

Long Live the Child Queen

When she searched for the translation, the search results pointed her in all kinds of wrong directions. The results showed modern day children's books and a Japanese anime show and silly YouTube videos. She searched again, this time adding keyword tags to her search, switching one out for another over and over again. Treasure. Gold. Pearls. Spanish.

Delta struck gold again when she added Spanish. The phrase "Isabel II" on the screen caught her eye. She, like everyone in Rey del Mar, Florida, knew who that was. The town's founder was her ex-husband, the former King of Spain, Francisco de Asís y Borbón, Duke of Cadiz. After their divorce was finalized, he fled for the Americas and founded her Florida town with his new love, Henri LaRocque. When Henri died, Francisco became a recluse and eventually fell into madness.

Local lore said he'd hidden his amassed treasure, believed to have been extorted from Isabel herself, somewhere in town. Some people believed in its existence, but since it hadn't been found in the 150 years since the town's founding, most never believed it ever existed and used the fact Francisco left mothering for their son as proof.

She waded through the search results, trying to find the most relevant links and absentmindedly playing with the coin hanging from her neck. One link highlighted the reign of Isabel, the child queen, crowned at age 3 when her father died, and how one coup after another influenced her reign. Another link dove into the marriage between Isabel and Francisco, how their marriage remained unconsummated and "their" children weren't actually his, how their divorce was inevitable, how they both indulged in extramarital affairs.

Article after article, she kept reading. She fell so far down the rabbit hole that she lost all recollection of time and startled when her brother called her name from the doorway.

"Yoo hoo, Delta," Dylan teased.

She jerked away from her computer and turned a vengeful glare at him for coming in her room without permission.

"You don't knock?"

"I did, a lot." He crossed his arms over his chest and leaned on the door frame. "Are you having an episode?"

She glanced back to the screen and decided she didn't want to tell him. Not yet. She didn't have anything concrete anyway, at least not about where the chain came from. She almost wanted to tell him about it but held back. It could be worth nothing, in which case, she'd feel silly. But what if it was worth a lot, what if it was important, what if it was just the start of something bigger? There might be something bigger. What if the treasure was real?

"Delta!"

"What?" she shouted back. Her mind was focusing on this discovery, and she was having trouble focusing on the now. She needed to center herself, so she closed her eyes and took a deep breath. She pressed her fingers onto the desk in front of her, one at a time. She listened for the air conditioning and the squawk of birds outside her window. "I'm fine. I was just doing some research. It's nothing important."

"If it's not important, how'd you lose track of the time?"

Her nose crinkled. "I never said I lost track of the time."

"No, but Mom did when she called asking why you were late for work." An grin snuck across his face, but it couldn't overtake the worry in his eyes.

A pit formed in her throat.

Dylan slunk from her room, and she quickly threw on clothes that she hadn't sweat all over. She'd wanted to shower and rest before work but missed the opportunity. Grabbing her backpack, she ran from the room and pulled her cell phone from the side pocket, noting the missed calls and texts.

How had she missed them all?

When Delta arrived at work, she knew she was in for it. She was over an hour late for her shift and missed her first performance entirely. Her bosses would not be happy about that. Mostly her mother. Her father would be understanding.

Her parents owned the Atlantic Aquatic Center, a facility that had pools for lessons, pools for the public, pools for Olympic training, and the largest professional mermaid training facility in the state. Her father, a serious but loving guy, worked in the office and ran the business operations while her mother, a high-strung woman, trained swimmers and mermaids and oversaw the day-to-day work in the actual pools.

On a good day, they would be judgy about her tardiness, but today must have already been a bad day. Her mother was silently seething as Delta strode past her and into the locker room to change, apologies dripping from her mouth.

After she changed into her costume and threw on her waterproof performance makeup, she wound her way to her mother's office and knocked hesitantly.

Her mother refused to look up from her paperwork. "We had to switch your shift with Adrienne. Check the schedule for your roles."

Knowing she disappointed her mother weighed on Delta. As with most firstborn children, she could be a little conscientious, but when she failed, it was usually in front of her mom. She hated the feeling of letting someone down, especially her mother.

Delta sulked toward the performers' entrance to the Clam, the performance pool where the public watched the mermaid shows. She leaned against the wall beside her friend Lucas, who would play the prince in this performance, and bumped him on the shoulder. In the show, she normally played the lead princess, because she was one of the best swimmers with an artificial tail, who falls for the prince, and together, they must overcome their differences. He'd been performing at the ACC almost as long as she had.

"Where you been?" he asked. His eyes lit up when he saw her.

"Just late."

"I hear you've been demoted."

"Yep, I'm not lead mermaid today. Works out for me. It means I don't have to kiss you." She ruffled his hair, and he blushed at the teasing.

"You know you're going to miss my artful prowess." He blew a kiss and threw her a wink. "Mrs. R. knows how to come up with a punishment, but why'd she have to punish me? I didn't do anything wrong."

She laughed, but it ended too soon. Isabel, Francisco, the treasure. It all weighed on her mind. But she suddenly remembered she had a connection to it all. Lucas was the grandson of Liam, the adopted child of Francisco and Henri. He might be able to tell her something her research hadn't.

"Do you remember those stories from when we were kids? The ones about the town treasure?" she asked, trying to play it cool.

"Of course, I do. My dad likes to tell them at every political function he can, how his great grandparents were Francisco and Henri LaRocque." He quirked his lips to the side. "He hates it when I remind him his grandpa was adopted by the LaRocques and wasn't actually descended from them."

Lucas's family were the town royals, almost literally. His great-grandfathers founded Mar del Rey, and his grandfather had become the town's first elected mayor. Each generation since has become mayor, and Lucas hated the legacy.

"Adopted is family, Lucas."

"I know, and I agree. But he always makes it seem like he should be recognized as a part of the old Spanish royal family or something. That's not how it works."

He had a point.

"Do you think the treasure is real?" she asked, biting her lip. She didn't want to let on how interested she was but was finding it hard to mask her curiosity.

"Do I think at one point Francisco, former King Consort of Spain, had gold and jewels and treasure, sure. I mean, even though Isabel was deposed, they weren't destitute. He still had money. Hell, he was still a duke. That title never went away." He pushed a hand through his wavy hair. "Do I think he was so distraught after Henri's death that he hid his amassed fortune and disappeared, never to be heard from again? No. I think the two of them spent it making their new life in Florida, founding the town, and building its original infrastructure. He was probably broke by the time he died."

"Hmm…" She thought about the necklace from this morning. If it wasn't part of a larger treasure, where did it come from? How did it wind up at the beach? "Your grandpa didn't get anything when Francisco died?"

"Not that I know of. My family mostly talks about the connection. They'd be bragging about any jewels or money they inherited if they got anything like that." He turned and checked the clock. "We should go. Our show is coming up, and you still need to put on your tail."

She started walking toward the tail storage, but he grabbed her arm. When she turned back, he nodded toward her neck.

"You should take that off before the show. You don't want to lose it in the tank."

Delta had forgotten she was wearing the coin; running late had really messed with her. But he was right. She'd be torn if she lost it, and the likelihood of finding it in the massive mermaid tank was low.

"Thanks, Lucas. You rock. I'm going to drop it in my locker. Don't let the show start without me."

After removing the necklace but before tucking it safely into her locker, she studied the coin. It really was something special. She could have sold it, but it had meant more to her. It was a link to the past. It sparked her interest in history. Plus, it gave her hope of recovering a massive treasure one day. Sometimes she felt forgettable, like life would pass her by and nobody would miss her when she was gone. But if she could uncover something of value, her name would be remembered forever. Maybe not around the world, but they'd remember her in town. The girl who found the lost treasure of Rey del Mar, Florida.

She flipped the coin over. The face of Isabel stared back as a memory struck her. She had walked the beach with her grandfather and brother the morning she found it. Dylan had complained he was tired and wanted to go home, but she'd had a compulsion to keep going. She knew there was something out there that morning, something to find, something precious. It wasn't long before the MetalLab vibrated, letting her know she was right. Then it beeped. She dug, refusing to let either of them help her because then it wouldn't be her find, and hers alone. It would have been a family discovery, and her name wouldn't be remembered. When she pulled the coin from the sand, she felt like she'd found the entire LaRocque fortune, not just a single coin.

She'd gone home that day and researched it, learning that the head on the coin was Isabel II, Queen of Spain.

She considered the chances that she'd find two random pieces of historical treasure on the same stretch of beach from the same country and the same era of history. Improbable, unless that town had a legend about a hidden treasure. Then she considered the odds that they both appeared at the same location without starting at the same place. Almost impossible, she guessed.

The thought sprung to her mind with as much force as a hurricane. The treasure was real, and it was still out there.

"Delta! Get out here now!" her mother's voice shouted into the locker room.

She gasped, left the necklace in her locker, and left to meet her mother in the hallway. She had zoned out again and was probably in a lot of trouble.

"What are you doing? The show was supposed to start five minutes ago."

"I had to put something in my locker. I'm headed to the Clam now."

"Go, before I pull you from the rest of the day's shows." Her mother pointed toward the performance pool and looked away.

A wave of guilt flushed over her. Delta hated disappointing her mother. She rushed down the hall, ran into tail storage, and grabbed her tail. She mumbled her apologies to Rocky, the choreographer, and the rest of the cast. Lucas shook his head at her, but his smirk let her know he wasn't really mad. She pulled the tail up her legs, secured it around her waist, and took a breath.

"Let's do this."

Delta sat at the desk in her room, tapping her finger beside her laptop, each tap growing louder as her tension grew. The next day had arrived before she knew it, but she was too keyed up and excited about her latest find to sleep. The time said it was far too late to still be up. Or way too early to be awake.

She was stumped. She knew there was a way to determine how the treasure she found would keep arriving on shore at the same location. She just couldn't figure out how to figure that out.

To clear her mind, she decided on a trip to the kitchen for a snack. After staring mindlessly inside for far too long, she pulled an orange from the refrigerator, and settled in at the table in the breakfast nook. She dug into the fruit with her nails. Tearing it apart helped to ease her racing mind.

She had concluded she needed help, another person to sound-board ideas off of. She was thinking of waking her brother when her dad bounded into the kitchen in his wetsuit. He liked to surf but didn't get out as much as he liked, and this morning, she was grateful he decided to go out.

"Hey, punkin," he said, kissing the top of her head as he passed her. He grabbed a granola bar from the pantry and a water bottle from the fridge. "Why're you up so early?"

"Couldn't sleep."

"Hmm." He tore open the granola bar and chomped down, taking half the bar in one bite.

"Dad?"

"Yeah?" he said around the food in his mouth.

"How… what… Ugh!" She ran her fingers through her hair and took a breath, her thoughts all jumbled. She took a breath. "I found something on the beach, on the same stretch of beach I found something else a while back."

"Should I be concerned about what these 'somethings' are?"

"No, just stuff. But the point is I found them on the same part of the beach."

"Okay?" He dragged out the word into multiple syllables as he joined her at the table.

"Is there a way to find out how they got there? Or, like, what caused them to show up on shore at the same location?"

"Probably, yeah." He stared at her, and she gestured for him to continue when he didn't. "Well, the water has patterns. You can look that up and follow the path."

"Water patterns?"

"Yes. The water moves in patterns or currents. But even more than that, you can look up what the patterns were on a specific day."

"Huh." She wondered if she could recall the exact date that she found the coin. She could look up the currents leading up to finding the chain, but she wanted a comparison. If they matched, she'd have a definitive place to start looking.

"And I see you're in another world already," her dad said with a teasing note. "If I'm not gone by the time your mother wakes, she'll put me to work, and I already don't get to surf as often as I'd like."

He kissed the top of her head and ruffled her hair before leaving.

She sat there just long enough to finish her orange then washed her hands and headed for her room. Her research had a new lead.

After she found the currents for the week leading up to when she found the chain, she decided to hunt for the other date. She couldn't recall it off the top of her head, and it was long before she started logging when she found things and where. She looked through her social media, hoping she posted a picture of it but knew she hadn't. It was too personal to show off. She didn't even have a photo of it on her phone, since she'd traded in a few phones since then.

Getting annoyed with herself for not having the information she needed at the ready, she either needed help or to lash out at someone over it. Who better than an annoying little brother?

Knocking on his door, she blew out a breath. When he didn't answer, she opened the door and found him still asleep across his bed. She jumped onto it and jostled him awake.

"Get out of here!" he shouted, pulling his pillow over his head.

"No," she said, settling onto the foot of the bed. "I need your help."

"Come back later," he grumbled.

"It can't wait." She wrestled the pillow from him and tucked it onto her lap.

"Monster," he spat while sitting up against the headboard.

"You love me, and you know it." She cheesed at him. "Now, do you remember when I found the coin?"

"That's what's so important you can't wait for me to wake up?"

"I haven't slept at all, so no, it couldn't wait. I can't get this out of my head and need your help."

He sobered quickly. "Really? Like at all?"

She couldn't hold back a yawn. "No, so help me please."

"I think you should call Dr. Fromm," he said, concern lacing his voice.

Dylan worried her OCD was manifesting again. She could usually control it with therapy and exercises, but the time between sessions had been growing each time. Sure, she had days where her mind forced her to continue an action or fall down a thought rabbit hole, like hiking the beach for longer than necessary or thinking so hard she missed phone calls. Sometimes her disorder yielded positive results, like finding the coin or discovering the chain. It was hard to give up the joy of discovery.

"I'm fine," she argued.

"You didn't sleep last night because you're obsessing over this find. It's happening again."

"No, it's not. I'll be able to sleep once I get this out of my head. Can you just help me please."

"Only if you call Dr. Fromm."

She groaned. "Fine. I will if you help me."

"What do you need?"

"It would be best if you could remember the date, but I doubt you would. Do you remember what else happened that weekend? I'm trying to pinpoint a time period."

Dylan rubbed his face with one hand and blew out a breath. "Um… Lito woke us while it was still dark. We picked up some donuts and took them to Carrigan Beach. We ate them while watching the sunrise before you got too impatient and started walking the shore with his metal detector."

"This isn't helping."

"Hold on, I'm thinking." He rubbed his temples. "I remember I wanted to leave. You made us walk for so long, we were practically in the dunes, and you know those are protected. You need to stay out of those!"

"Yeah, I do. Promise." She made a cross over her heart.

"Then the MetalLab started beeping, and you flipped out. Wouldn't even let Lito help you dig. 'It's my discovery,' you said, like you didn't use his equipment to find it. Technically, he should've gotten a piece of that thing."

She threw the pillow at him. "Can you stay on topic, please?"

He glared at her. "If you want my help, I'm going to tell the story my way."

"Fine."

"So…"

"What?"

"I'm thinking!" he growled. "I remember coming home, and you locked yourself in your room. You didn't even want to show Mom and Dad the coin, but Lito made you. Then I... Oh! I played video games with Tatum because he had just gotten the PS4 for his birthday."

"When's his birthday?"

"I remember now. He had his party the night before, but I can't recall if it was actually on his birthday or just the weekend near his birthday. Does that help?"

"It would help if you'd tell me his birthday."

"I don't know. Sometime in early July? He usually has his party around Independence Day. I remember because there's usually fire-works. Man, his mom is cool like that." While he was reminiscing, Delta stormed from the room. Dylan shouted after her, "You're welcome!"

Armed with a date, Delta researched the currents around the time she found the coin and found similarities between her discoveries. In the days leading up to both, a heavy rainstorm or hurricane had come through. That was probably important, she mused, to knock the treasure loose from wherever they'd been so they could flow with the current to the beach. The next similarity she found was the water patterns circulated from Carrigan Beach back to the LaRocque Bluffs.

Could Francisco have hidden his treasure in the bluffs he named for the love of his life? It would make a silly sort of sense, leaving them for Henri to look after for all those years. How could she figure out the proper leadoff location?

She had a treasure hunt to plan.

It rarely rained in Florida during the winter. Though the temperatures were quite chilly for the locals, it only dipped below freezing temps a few days during the season. Then came a day in early March where the temperatures lowered, and a storm rolled in.

Delta was at work when the rain began. She'd been assigned to the public pool that day, covering for one of the lifeguards who called in sick. And, while everybody else had grumbled and bemoaned having to get out of the pool due to the inclement weather, she was the lone person with a smile stretched across her face.

This incoming storm meant she could put her plan into action. It was all she'd been able to think about since she'd found the chain a month earlier. How to plan the perfect plan. How to perfect the perfect plan. How to afford the perfect plan.

After finding the likely water patterns to wind up on Carrigan Beach, Delta figured out a method of following the path toward the dunes. She decided on five launch points across the bluffs and figured out a way to watch the water patterns in real time. After deciding on her path forward, she was concerned about the cost. Sure, she had a job, but she wanted to be able to afford her plan and not borrow from anyone. In case she found something, she didn't want to owe her big discovery to someone else. Luckily, she figured out cheap ideas, found everything she needed online, and ordered her materials for less than $40. She couldn't believe her luck.

Once the pool area was clear of stragglers and her closing duties were complete, she headed toward the locker room. She changed and put on street clothes and sneakers, stuffing her flip flops, swimsuit, and towel at the bottom of her pool bag. In her haste to leave, she tumbled into her mother outside the locker room. Her brother leaned against the wall across the hallway and piqued an eyebrow at her clumsiness.

"Oof." She took a step back and checked her mother was alright. "Sorry, Mom. Guess I was distracted."

Her mother brushed her hands down her sides and straightened. "It's alright. I have to stay for a partner meeting. Can you drive your brother home?"

Panic hit her suddenly, though she wasn't sure why—she wasn't doing anything wrong—so she smiled and nodded.

Her mother kissed her temple. "Thanks, Sweetheart. We have to meet with Amy about our marketing strategy and Rocky about changing the choreography for the mermaid shows. She wants to do this whole big thing. Doesn't matter. Just take him home, drive safe, and your dad and I'll bring home dinner after the meeting."

"Sounds good," she said, hoisting her bag higher onto her shoulder. "Hear Rocky out. The routine is getting stale."

"That's only because you do the same routine multiple times a day. It doesn't look stale to the audience, who usually only see it once or, at most, once per day."

"Yeah, yeah," she mumbled, heading down the hallway toward the staff parking lot. "You coming, Dylan?"

Dylan ran after her and caught up, struggling with his bag.

"How's training going?" she asked.

Since it was a family business, everyone worked at the aquatic center. Lito started it with their Abuelita years ago, before their mother was even born. Then their dad married into it, helping to run the business part so their mom could keep her more creative role. Delta worked as a lifeguard, a mermaid, and occasionally a swim teacher, when she needed to fill in for a more senior employee. Now that he was 14, Dylan was training to play the role of the prince in the mermaid shows and as a lifeguard, though he couldn't officially lifeguard until his 15th birthday.

"It's alright." He kicked his bag in front of him, hanging from his lowered arm. "Kind of boring."

"Yeah, the princes don't really have a big role. People really come to see the mermaids."

"Yep."

They ran across the parking lot, ducking their heads beneath their bags, though they still got drenched, especially since Delta's passenger seat was full of junk so Dylan waited in the rain while she cleared it. Finally, she cleared the seat, and he climbed inside.

"What is all this?" he asked, pulling things from a canvas bag she'd thrown onto the backseat.

"Don't worry about it," she said, tugging the bag toward her. She pulled out an X-Acto knife and a package of rubber duckies. "Do me a favor and cut the bottoms of these open. I need them big enough to stuff something inside."

"You're so weird." Though he judged her, he took the tool and toys and did as she asked.

As she wove her way around town, he worked quietly.

"Where are we going?" he asked.

"I have something I need to take care of quick. It won't take long."

"This for that secret project of yours?"

"Yes."

"Are these ducks part of it?"

"Yep. When you're done cutting them open, take the keyring trackers out of the baggie. They're all charged up, so click the button on the side to turn them on and stuff one in each duck."

"Then what?"

"Then close the ducks with a piece of duct tape. Each duck should have a different color. That way I can keep track of them."

She pulled up to the first stop along the bluffs where she believed was the likely start of the first water pattern and grabbed one of the ducks, noting the color of tape covering the bottom. She ran into the rain, leaving her brother in the running car, and across the bluff.

Should she drop the duckie or throw it, she wondered, before finally tossing it underhanded into the water.

The rain pelted down her face, her hair draping down her cheeks and neck. Her sweatshirt clung to her and grew heavier the longer she watched the duck disappear. When she turned toward the vehicle, her brother stared at her wide-eyed.

She tucked herself back behind the steering wheel, dried her hands with her towel, and pulled a paper map of the town from the canvas bag. She wrote the color of the duckie beside one of the five circles she had drawn across the bluffs. Green. Then she handed the map to her brother and put the car back into gear.

"What's with the rubber ducks?" he asked after stopping several more times, tossing the blue, pink, and orange ducks from other locations.

"I'm using them to watch the water patterns," she explained, though keeping the real reason for her research private.

"Water patterns." He grumbled. "Since when have you been the least bit interested in them?"

They pulled over for the fifth and final stop. She was cold and shivering—the heat in the car was blasting at full strength, much to Dylan's dislike—but she only had a short window to finish. Rainstorms in Florida didn't always last very long.

"Since Dad told me about them, I've been learning all that I can. They're pretty interesting."

"Hm..." He crossed his arms. "Right. This has nothing to do with that coin you found and getting me to remember that weekend?"

She side-eyed him. There was no reason not to tell him, but she wasn't sure if she should. "I'll tell you when there's something to tell."

She climbed out of the car and ran through the downpour. Standing on the edge of the final overhang of the LaRocque Bluffs, she tossed the purple duck into the water and watched it fall. The trackers had a passive battery life of two months, but since she was using them actively, they would only last for about a week. She hoped they landed on the beach by then, or she'd have to do the testing all over again.

As she crawled back into the car, her brother had a concerned look on his face.

"When's the last time you spoke with Dr. Fromm?"

Delta considered that.

"If you can't remember, it's been too long, Delta," he said. He threw his hands up. "This, right here, is not healthy. You're following an obsession—this is an obsession! —and it's going to hurt you in the end."

"I am fine. This is just research. I'm not obsessed."

"Yes, you are," he sighed, turning to stare out the passenger window, "and it won't only hurt you when it ends."

She thought about her last episode, when she'd gotten so obsessed with conspiracy theories after finding a flash drive on the beach and had to be hospitalized. She'd been gone for two months and couldn't recall the entire first month she was there. That was the last thing she wanted to happen.

"It won't go that far because I'm fine."

It was a Sunday morning when Delta crossed off the purple duck's launch area on her map. The duck had arrived on the beach sometime overnight, according to her tracking app. The other four ducks had either landed way off course or didn't make landfall at all. She had a current to follow.

Since she had the morning off work, she didn't want to wait to start her search. She put on her swimsuit, then pulled her wetsuit over it. She stuffed her backpack with everything she'd need for a day on the water—a tank, shorts, a sand-sifter scoop, a trowel, her snorkel, flipper fins, and her goggles. Snacks and water bottles were things she'd planned to grab from the kitchen on her way out of the house.

As she headed toward her bedroom door, Dylan's concerns replayed in her mind. He was worried about her, and she appreciated that, but it was unnecessary. She wanted to do something to put his mind at ease, so she wrote him a note.

Dyl,

I'll tell you about everything

when I get home tonight. Promise.

–Delta

She slipped the letter beneath his door and headed toward the garage. She needed to borrow the small motorboat her dad used sometimes and hoped he wouldn't miss it today. Instead of taking her old beater car, she borrowed Lito's old truck and hitched the boat to the back. He'd understand. Besides, it wasn't like he'd be stranded. She left her own car for him.

The entire drive, Delta felt a pull, something tugging her forward. A calling to lead the search. She knew she had to be the one to find the treasure.

By the time she got the boat onto the water, a lot more time had passed than she'd expected. It was easier to get the boat ready when she had help, especially since she'd never done it alone. Either her dad or abuelo did most of the work. She didn't have much time before she had to head home, but she wanted to at least start her search, to get onto the right path.

From the boat ramp, she used the motor to take her out to the bluffs, wanting to use the current to her advantage. She figured the water would guide her as it moved, less forceful swimming for her. When she got as close to the bluffs as she dared, she dropped anchor, pulled on her goggles, grabbed her snorkel, and dove into the water.

The problem with her search, she soon realized, was how deep the water was at the bluffs. Even with the sun out at full force, she still couldn't see the floor bottom. If there was treasure, that's where it would be. It's not like it'd be floating around in the water. The search was doomed if she couldn't see.

Little mini dives, she decided. All her years at the ACC made her a strong swimmer. Mermaids had to stay underwater for so long. She could find a spot, take a large gulp of oxygen, and dive as far as she could on one breath. Then, she would surface and do it again in another spot.

After the sun hit its highest point, Delta had been diving for some time and knew she'd have to turn in soon. She had work, and her search was proving useless. She'd have to come back with her SCUBA gear and swim the entire path along the floor bottom. There was no way she'd find anything with her current plan of being a human bobber.

But before she made her final climb for air, something caught her eye. Could it be a piece of treasure, something to prove she was on the right course of action?

She swam closer toward the floor. Her lungs begged her to return to the surface, but she needed to see for herself. A compulsion took over, and she was a slave to it. She couldn't turn back now if she wanted to.

A glimmer of light shone off of something. Whatever it was had a reflective surface. She pointed her swimming directly for it but didn't seem to be getting any closer.

Her lungs burned in her chest, desperately begging her to take a breath, but she fought the feeling. She'd felt it before, when she was training to be a mermaid. She had learned how to go for minutes without oxygen and routinely held her breath for three to four minutes underwater. She reminded herself it was just excess CO_2 in her lungs. It had no place to go, so it sat there until she exhaled. But she couldn't do that, she needed the remaining oxygen in her lungs to keep her going.

At this depth, her arms and legs were growing sore from pushing through the pressure. That wasn't something she had to deal with at work. It was hindering her dive here.

Her head grew light as a wave of dizziness struck her, bobbing along with the flow of the water. She had trouble keeping her gaze steady. All she wanted to do was close her eyes and hold onto something solid, but there was nothing here. Too far from the cliffs. Too far from the boat. Too far from the floor.

Delta focused on the glimmer and pushed herself further. She knew, in her bones, that she'd done it. She found the treasure, Francisco's treasure, her treasure.

As her vision blackened, she knew she'd done it. She'd be remembered forever.

Siren's Song

Katharine Bost

As soon as the song is finished playing, my manager clicks the space-bar on the keyboard. Mr. Rogers gives me a big smile, toothpick still stuck in his teeth.

"I think this is a hit," he tells me. "Bigger than 'Roses.' Mark my words."

Beside him, my agent and the recording studio manager nod their heads. It's a catchy tune. Should be top ten within the first week that we release it, maybe even number one. Most of my singles are.

I don't say that to brag. It's not like people can help it. My voice is just… catchy. The melody makes people want to dance or blare the song while they drive down the street. As *Rolling Stone* said, *Cassidy Mare couldn't write a bad song if she tried.*

Not that I would *try* to write a bad song ever, but it's still nice to hear.

As Mr. Rogers talks about the logistics, I drag my finger along the pearl on my necklace. It's simple, not very flashy, but is everything when it comes to my success as a musician. My success as a person, really.

"Got all that, Deron?" Mr. Rogers asks my personal assistant.

Deron is new. And it shows. He never writes the correct notes and he has a profusive sweating problem, but he's also the nephew of my old personal assistant and she recommended him highly. He's fresh out of college, barely older than me, and definitely green around the gills.

"Um, yeah, I've got that. Um, could you repeat the last bit, though?" Deron wipes his forehead with the sleeve of his button-down, which stains the fabric with his sweat. He'd be adorable if it weren't for his inability to do anything correctly.

Mr. Rogers sighs. He gestures for us to wrap this up. "Cassidy needs to be home for her Epsom salt bath in twenty. Think you can handle getting her back in one piece, Deron?"

Deron startles, dropping the pen he was holding. "Me?"

I close my eyes and wonder if it's too late to put out an ad for a new personal assistant. It's only been three days, but Deron has done nothing but bungle everything. Honestly, he stresses me out more than learning the new choreography for a show. And that's with my feet not being as smooth as other people's. Sometimes I dance like they're still conjoined. Comedic for my dance instructors during rehearsal, but stressful that it might happen onstage during a performance.

Just yesterday, Deron managed to mix up my morning and afternoon teas, which grated my throat during rehearsals. He's supposed to be paying attention to the small details, but he can't even get the big ones right. At least he tries, I suppose, and anytime he does something inherently wrong, he overcompensates to correct it. Like when he forgot to bring my coffee this morning, so he brought two coffees this afternoon.

I know I should give him time to learn the tricks of the trade, but it felt like Eve knew everything instinctually. How can someone related to her be such a polar opposite? Maybe I was just spoiled since she was my first personal assistant and always seemed to do everything right. Maybe this is how personal assistants really are.

Mr. Rogers is lecturing Deron, who looks like a fish out of water. He blinks rapidly, nodding his head, saying "yes, sir" and "no, sir" over and over again.

It's not imperative that I have an Epsom salt bath, but it reminds me of being in the ocean, and I like to experience that at least once a day, preferably more. It reminds me of home.

Deron stands up, shoving his notepad into his briefcase. It falls out, and he struggles to zip it into the satchel. He slings it around his shoulder, and it knocks a cup of water over onto the table. He clears his throat.

"Are you ready, Ms. Mare?"

The Epsom salt bath was refreshing. I took the time to run through some of my old melodies and jot song lyrics down on a worn notepad.

There's a song on the precipice, but I can't figure out the right words or the right order. Touching my lucky pearl doesn't help, either. It feels like there needs to be something else that reveals it to me.

I didn't have too long to soak in the bath, though, since I have another signing tonight. Just stayed long enough for the water to refresh me and hold me over until tomorrow.

Tonight's signing is at a record store downtown, only for a select number of fans. The ones who have listened to "Roses" nonstop and downloaded all my albums. The ones we're rewarding for being such avid admirers. We capped the number at thirty, and all I have to do is sign autographs and take pictures. I might have to perform an acoustic song or two, but Deron is supposed to let me know.

Which isn't the most promising thing I've ever thought, so maybe I should clear it with Mr. Rogers first. He'll likely know more than Deron.

As I'm dialing, there's a knock on my front door. My house is small for the level of success I've had in the music industry, and I can hear the knock from my room. Mr. Rogers will have to wait, which works out well because he doesn't answer. Maybe he'll call me back soon.

Despite having the best security, I've learned to always look through the peephole first, in case someone dangerous is on the other side. But it's just Deron.

He's smoothing his hair back and waving his shirt for better air circulation when I open the door.

"Cassidy, hey," he says, his voice cracking. "I mean—Ms. Mare. I was just, um, admiring your front door."

I ignore that. "Do you want to come in?"

He nods, and I move aside for him to enter the house. Since he's only been my personal assistant for a few days, he hasn't been inside my house before. I expect a comment from him, though I'm not sure what.

"It's very aquatic," he says, noting the many aquariums I have spread throughout the abode. Most of the knickknacks around are items you'd find in a beach house, and the walls are painted a warm yellow. It, like Epsom salt baths, reminds me of home.

"Thanks," I say. "Are you here to discuss the signing tonight?"

"Signing?" His brows furrow. "Oh! Right. The signing. Yeah. That's why I'm here."

I might as well not have a personal assistant at this rate.

"Yeah, I'm here to collect you for that. Are you ready?" He checks his watch. "I guess we have a few hours, but Mr. Rogers wanted you to get to the venue early. Scope stuff out."

"Am I performing?"

He looks confused again. "I don't think so. Should you be?"

"Probably," I say, trying not to get annoyed that he hasn't set anything up. "The fans will want an intimate performance."

"Intimate?"

"Acoustic." This is clearly his first job, I remind myself. He's just new. He'll learn.

"Right. Is this something I should have set up with the venue?"

I nod my head very slowly.

"Right," he says again. "I'll work on that while you get dressed. It'll be fine."

"But I haven't rehearsed anything," I say, which is just as much my fault as it is his. I have been so caught up in the new single that I haven't prepared for this meet and greet.

"Well, play your new song and play 'Roses.' They'll love that, and they'll love being the first to hear your new song," he says.

"The label company won't want me playing it early unless we get their permission," I say. "Unless you've already cleared it with them?"

His eyes widen. "Cleared it? Oh, yeah, duh, I cleared it already. Definitely. You're golden."

I'm totally not golden, and I'm definitely not performing that song without the label's explicit approval.

I rub my hands down my face, exasperated. "Just go wait in the car while I get dressed. Hair and makeup meeting us at the venue?"

"Um, sure, sure."

I sigh. Guess that's up to me to coordinate, too.

Hair and makeup takes about two hours, and then people are showing up outside the venue doors. Deron thought it would be a good idea to start the night off with a couple of songs and then proceed to the meet and greet part of the night, and for once, I agree with him.

Before performing, I drink hot lemon water to soothe my throat and touch the pearl at the base of my neck. It pulses beneath my fingertips, ready to give me the power to serenade.

The room is packed when I go out to the stage. I don't feel nervous performing in front of people anymore, and instead thrive on the attention. It's much different than my life in the sea, when it was a different concert every night, but I was never the best performer. Here, on land, no one compares to me.

"Thank you all for being here tonight," I say into the microphone. I'm seated on a stool with an acoustic guitar on my lap, and I strum through a few chords to get the tune right. "This is really special to me because I don't get to do intimate performances often, so I'm happy I get to share this moment with you."

The crowd of course cheers at that, but it's not the same kind of atmosphere as one of my concerts. It's much more mellow, though I can still feel the eyes of every person and their cameras facing me.

Since it's the crowd's favorite, I wait to perform "Roses" last. Unlike a regular concert, no one dares to sing along with me. The only voice in the room is mine, and it echoes off the walls. The aisles have been cleared of vinyl records and CDs to make way for chairs and people to sit.

The audience erupts into clapping and cheers once I play the final notes. In the back of my mind, I think about how the sound was tinny since Deron didn't hook up the right speakers, but I try not to worry about that now. The performance is done and it went well, and that's what matters.

I wave my hand to show my appreciation, and then Deron is guiding me to the table where I'll sign autographs and take pictures with fans. His hand is sweaty against the small of my back, and I try not to cringe from his touch.

"That was great," he says to me, sounding nervous. "I've never heard a voice that beautiful before."

"Thanks," I say as I sit down behind the table. "Did you get enough Sharpies for me?"

"In all different colors. Every color of the rainbow," he says, though I've specifically said I only like signing in metallic silver or aqua.

It's fine. I can autograph in fuchsia, too. Dad always told me to pick my battles, and this seems like a small one in the grand scheme of things.

The first few fans come and go in a blur. I sign their names, take pictures with them, and then they're on their merry way. Deron is there beside me to make sure no one gets too handsy with me, which I appreciate. He's had to restrain three people already, and even though he doesn't do a great job of making sure they leave me alone, the point is that he tries.

Thirty. Only thirty total, I remind myself. It's not that I don't like meeting fans, but I just feel like so many things could go wrong or I might say the wrong thing and lose a fan forever. It's much more personal than just singing in front of a microphone. These are actual, real people who have real feelings. What if I say something that hurts them?

The last fan hugs me. I don't normally allow full frontal hugs just because they're so personal, but I'm so glad that it's the last fan I don't have any room for complaints. Deron is there to make sure the hug doesn't last too long, and then the fan leaves. I don't remember much about him or any of the fans, really, which probably says a lot about me. I'm just glad it's done and I didn't do anything embarrassing.

As I'm sitting back down, feeling overly tired for some odd reason, I realize something is missing. I touch my index finger to the base of my neck, but my pearl is no longer there.

It's gone.

My method of singing—of being *human*—is gone. And I have no idea where it could be.

Immediately I scour the vicinity. Maybe the clasp broke and it fell off somewhere. It had to have happened after I performed, or else I wouldn't have been able to sing that well. So that means at some point between sitting down and meeting with the last fan, I lost my pearl necklace.

"I think that went rather well," Deron says. "My first event. A success, if I may say so myself."

"This is a tragedy," I whisper, still groping at my neck as if that will make my pearl appear.

"A tragedy? No, it went great! Everyone was in tears when you sang

'Roses.' I could feel myself going misty-eyed."

"My necklace is gone," I say, my voice hoarse. Oh, no. Is that how my voice is going to sound from now on? What else will happen? What other horrors await me?

"Oh, the pretty pearl. What a shame," Deron says. "Was it sentimental? Did one of your parents give it to you?"

"My dad did," I say. "There's nothing else like it. I need to find it. I have to find it." I stand up abruptly, but the movement makes me woozy.

Deron catches me by the arms. His palms are clammy. "Hey, take it easy," he says. "We'll find it. It has to be around here somewhere."

"Unless someone took it—then I'll never get it back," I say miserably.

"It must have been pretty special to you," Deron says.

"You have no idea."

But he's about to find out.

The first change is subtle. I barely notice it. The morning after I lost my pearl, I wake up to see the skin at my toes has webbed. It's a little horrifying, yes, but I can cover it with socks and shoes. No one is the wiser.

It's the threat of what is to come that makes me the most nervous. I have to get the pearl back. Until I retrieve it, I won't be able to perform. And worse than that, I won't be human for much longer.

It was a simple spell from the sea witch. Trade my immortality and fins for a singing career and legs. It's worked out for me the last several years, but that was before I lost the thing that bound me to the contract. Now that the pearl isn't touching my skin, I can feel myself slipping back into the ocean. Back to being a mermaid.

How long until I become inhuman completely? What will the record company tell my fans? What will the media think?

I'm contemplating my demise, thinking of the awful stories they'll spin about me (she joined a cult, she became a scientologist, she kidnapped orphans and moved to Antarctica) when there's a knock on my door.

It's Deron. Again. And I don't want to see him. He's probably here to remind me about the photoshoot I have later today (if he even remembers), but I can't go to a photoshoot looking like this. What if they make me take my socks off?

"Hey, Cassidy," he says. There's a satchel slung over his shoulder and he's wearing a blazer today. It's the most official he's looked since he took over the position. "Er, Ms. Mare. Ready to take on the day?"

I cough. "Actually, no. I must be coming down with something." I cough again, this time more forcefully.

He recoils slightly. "You're right. Your voice does sound a little hoarse. Is it your throat?"

I wheeze, and he backs up. "It's everything, really. I just feel under the weather."

"That's no good," he says, pulling his phone out. "I'll have to postpone filming for the new music video."

"That's tomorrow," I remind him. "Today is the photoshoot with *Vogue*."

He stares at me, eyes wide. "Oh. Right. Yeah, I'll have to call *Vogue*." He pauses. "I don't want to call *Vogue*. Any way you can fake feeling okay? I'm sure the photoshoot won't take that long."

As he's talking, I glance down at my hands. Like my feet, they've started to web. I watch the skin knit together and bind my fingers. I have to get Deron off my property now.

"I don't think I can fake it," I say, my voice rising in pitch. Panicking. I'm absolutely panicking, and Deron needs to leave so I can figure out a solution on my own.

Unfortunately, Deron follows my gaze. His wide eyes widen even further, and he takes a step back.

"Your hands! Is this that new foot and mouth disease I've heard about? I thought that only affected toddlers and infants," he says, covering his mouth. He glances down at his hands, then breathes a sigh of relief, likely because there are still spaces between his fingers.

"It's called hand, foot, and mouth disease, and that's not—ugh, that's not what it is," I say, a little exasperated. Of all the people I wanted to trust with my secret, Deron was not one of them. But I have little choice, since I'm turning back into a mermaid as we speak, and I need an ally to help me get my pearl back.

I have no idea where it went, but Deron is as good of a help as any.

Okay, fine, he's the only option I have. He can at least go out in public, which is more than I can say about myself.

Except he's shifting his gaze from my fingers to my toes, and that's when I realize I'm not wearing socks yet.

"Your—your feet," he says.

"I know."

"They're... webbed. Have they always been webbed? Have I just not noticed this? I would think that I would have noticed this."

"It's new," I say, then realize that's not exactly the truth. "Well, not completely new, but a recent development. Can you come in?"

He fumbles with his phone, and it slides from his grip, clattering to the ground with a crack. The screen is definitely shattered. As he bends to pick it up, he does so quickly, likely to avoid being near my feet longer than he has to be.

I take a deep breath, praying to the sea god for patience. "Today, Deron."

"Right, right." He pockets his phone, not even checking for damage. "I can come in. Totally. This is... this is fine. I'll go inside, and you won't eat me, and it'll be okay."

"I'm not going to eat you."

"Steal my voice, then?"

"I don't want your voice."

"My youth?"

"You're older than me."

Deron opens his mouth, likely to grace me with another one of his stupid theories, but then he shuts it. "Okay. I can come in."

He moves past me, his shoulders shaking, and enters the house. His shoes drag across the floor as he crosses the threshold, and I shut the door behind him.

"So, what are you? What disease do you have? Is it contagious?"

Sighing, I rub my eyes. He's my only choice, I remind myself. I wish it could be someone like Mr. Rogers, but he likely wouldn't believe me, and would probably have me institutionalized. At least with Deron, I know he won't sell my secret to the media, but that's likely because he wouldn't know who to call for that.

"I don't have a disease," I say. "And it's not contagious. You're safe."

"I don't feel safe."

"Remember the pearl? The one I lost at the meet and greet last night?"

He nods, his hands vibrating at his sides.

There's no way to say this easily, so I rip the Band-Aid off. Either he believes me or he doesn't, but he's the best choice I have. The more time I waste, the more this will affect me. The more I'll turn back into a mermaid—time is of the essence.

"The pearl kept me human and helped me maintain my voice."

Deron swallows audibly. "Human?" he whispers. "Then what are you?"

"A siren," I say. "Or a mermaid. Whichever one you want. I come from the sea."

He gestures to my hands and feet. "That would explain the webbing, I suppose. But... why are you here?"

"To be a singer," I say. "I didn't stick out under the sea, but I knew I could make it big up here. And I have. Everyone loves my voice and music."

"Because you're a *siren*, oh my gosh," Deron says. It looks like he's about to faint. He presses the back of his hand to his forehead and takes a deep breath. "I'm talking to a *siren*."

"Yes. A siren who needs your help."

His attention snaps to me. "My help? What could you possibly want from me? I thought you said you weren't going to eat me."

"Sirens don't eat people, they lure them to their deaths and drown them," I say. "Haven't you read any mythology?"

Sweat trickles down Deron's brow. "It's hot in here. Is it hot in here to you?" He looks around. "The only water I see are in the aquariums. Are you going to make me drown in those?"

"No," I say, feeling that exasperation from earlier. "I couldn't even if I wanted to since my voice doesn't work right anymore. I can't sing."

"But you can speak?"

"It's not the same thing."

"Ah, I see," he says, but it doesn't look like he does. He shrugs out of his blazer and hangs it on the doorhandle. Pockets of sweat ring his armpits on his maroon button-down. He unbuttons the top button, as if that'll help him breathe easier.

We stand in silence for several moments. I wait for him to faint, possibly burst into tears, but he remains stoic aside from the profuse sweating.

"I think it goes without saying that this is a secret," I say, just in case he needed reminding. "No telling anyone, including Mr. Rogers. But especially no media."

"Did my aunt know?" he asks.

"No one except me. And now you. So, we have to keep it between us, or else."

"What's the 'or else'?"

I close my eyes. "I don't know, but it would be bad. Besides, it's not like anyone would believe you that the world's biggest pop star happens to be a mermaid."

He nods, considering this. "Fair point."

"Do we have a deal that this remains a secret between us? No telling anyone, even your aunt?"

"I can't believe she never figured it out," he says.

"The pearl makes me very convincing. But now that it's gone, so are all my talents, and so is my ability to appear human. I need it back."

Deron seems to consider this. He watches me carefully before finally nodding once. "What do you need from me, then?" he asks, and I could have hugged him.

The first thing Deron and I do is compile a list of the attendants for the meet and greet, including any staff. We've narrowed the timing down to during the actual meeting of the fans, since I wouldn't have been able to perform without the pearl. That means it had to have been stolen after I played the songs.

"I can't believe someone would steal your necklace," Deron says to me over a cup of coffee. We're sitting in my kitchen, surrounded by the soothing sounds of the ocean. I have my feet in a foot bath filled with salt to help mimic the ocean, but I can still feel my body itching to submerge itself fully in the saltwater. It's not enough, and I even found a scale on my leg earlier that morning.

"They probably just wanted a part of me," I say, though I'm also annoyed someone would steal it. What could they possibly want it for? To put it up for auction? To put in a display case?

"I've checked eBay and the other auction sites," Deron says. "No sign of it. I think they would've put it up by now if they intended to sell it."

"It would be too easy," I say. "We could've gotten the law involved and forced them to give it back."

"Or bought it outright, if worse came to worst," he says. "Which is stupid since it's yours to begin with."

I look through the names on the papers in front of us. Some people live nearby, but a lot don't. A lot of people traveled from all over the country to see me perform. They'll be harder to track down. This could take weeks, and I don't know if I have weeks.

If it comes down to it, I might have to rely on Deron to get the pearl back, because I might have to be in the ocean before long.

I rub my arms, feeling the raised, hardened skin that will soon transform into scales. I'm working on borrowed time.

Deron seems to notice my concern. He reaches out and touches my hand. His fingers are sweaty, as usual. "Hey, it'll be okay. We'll find it and no one will ever know. You'll be back and touring in no time."

"That's the thing," I say. "I'm supposed to release the new single soon, and the record company will expect me to do promotions for it. I can't do promotions while I'm incapacitated like this. It's been bad enough getting everyone off my case the last few days, pretending to be sick. Sooner or later, Mr. Rogers is going to catch on, or try to make me work despite being sick. Time is money here, and I'm wasting it."

Deron squeezes my hand and then lets go, opting to flip through the pages. He settles on the first one, running his finger along the name at the top. "We'll just have to visit every person, then. And fast."

"Mr. Rogers is going to notice that I'm sick but still flying across the country," I say. "And I can't go out in public like this. Who knows how soon it'll be before the scales sprout? Before my legs conjoin again?"

My feet are pruned in the foot bath, and I move them around a little bit while they're still separated. The movement splashes water up the sides of the bath, but not outside of it. Deron stares at the papers, as if they will give him the answers.

"Well, we have to do something," he says. "Maybe we can start with the people who live locally and drive to them? I have a car we can fit this foot bath in."

"I'm going to need more than a foot bath soon," I say. "I'll need a full tub."

The next morning, the beginnings of scales have sprouted down my legs. They aren't full-blown scales yet, but they itch and need water poured on them constantly. Otherwise, they dry out, and that's a new shade of uncomfortable.

Mr. Rogers calls me twice, but I ignore both. My voice is starting to go out, and although it might be believable for me to sound sick, I don't want to talk to him. What if he notices something is up? What if he insists on coming over to check on me? It's better to let Deron tell him what's going on. He seems able to handle that, at least.

Deron comes over late in the morning. He seems excited when I open the door, but that excitement fades when he sees the scales on my legs.

"It's spreading," I tell him, and he nods.

"I bought a van," he says. "One that can fit a freezer box in it. I even filled it with water, so you can come along with me."

"Isn't that dangerous?"

"Yeah, I'll try not to get pulled over," he says. "Otherwise, I'll have a lot of explaining to do."

"Having a freestanding tub in your backseat will be the least of your worries," I say, thinking of how Deron of all people would explain to having a mermaid in his van.

He smiles at that. It's a nice smile, with dimples framing each side of his mouth. His teeth are straight and white, and the grin makes him appear much cuter than his serious or panicked face.

"I guess we'll just have to not get caught."

The first two houses we go to are busts. Deron goes in alone under the premise of being my personal assistant and looking for someone to star in my upcoming music video. It's definitely something we can make work, I just have to clear it with the label eventually, but they wouldn't mind that. It's the kind of heartwarming thing they go crazy for: rewarding fans for loving my music.

"I looked all around," Deron says, "but I couldn't find anything."

It's starting to seem hopeless, I think as I swirl around in the tub. Then I start wondering if it would really be that big of a deal to hang up my fins and retreat to the ocean. I had a good run, had several big hits and won a few Grammys. Wasn't that enough? Maybe it'd have to be.

I'm sure my dad would welcome me home with open arms. I wouldn't be the best musician anymore, but that seems so small in the grand scheme of things.

As soon as Deron returns from the fourth house, he notices something has changed in my demeanor.

"What is it?" he asks as he buckles his seatbelt. He doesn't turn the car on, instead takes his time striking out the next name on our list.

"Would it be the worst thing to throw the towel in?" I say. "I mean, think about it. This way, I don't have to fade to black or get old in the public's eye. I can just leave while I'm at my most successful. It could be a thrilling mystery, too, with people wondering whatever happened to Cassidy Mare. But no one will ever know the truth—except you."

The muscle in Deron's jaw twitches. "But what about me?" he asks. "What about being your personal assistant?"

"You could be someone else's personal assistant."

He laughs at that, but it doesn't sound natural. It sounds sad. "No, I couldn't. I'm not even good at being your personal assistant. I never get the dates right and I can't figure out who to call about photoshoots. My phone is constantly ringing and I never answer it because I'm afraid of what the person is going to say. You're going to lose so many endorsements because of me."

"I was wondering why my days seemed quieter recently," I say by means of a joke. It makes Deron smile a little, but I can tell he's still bothered. "Look, it's fine. It's your first week on the job. You'll get the hang of it."

"My aunt made this life sound so glamorous," he says glumly. "She could retire early and spend time with family because of the salary, which is something I wanted to do. She made it all sound so easy, I thought I could do it. But it's not as easy as she made it out to be."

"To be fair, your aunt was unnaturally good at her job," I say. "It's hard to fill her shoes."

He stares down at the papers in his hands, and I skim my hands across the water. Even though it's a full tub, it hasn't spilled at all. He had the back seats removed so he could fit this freezer tub in it, and it's spacious. He might not be the best personal assistant, but he's definitely thoughtful. That has to count for something.

"I need this job," Deron says. "I'm not really good at anything else. I mean, I'm not really good at this, either, but it's what I can do. I have the opportunity, and I think the means to be good at it, I just need time."

I don't remind him that we don't really have much time if we don't find the pearl. I'm sure he already knows, and reminding him would just stress him out more.

"Okay," I say. "We'll keep searching. I won't give up."

That seems to placate him. He smiles again, and I look down at the water, a faint heat trapped in my cheeks. It's just because he's being nice and honestly, I'm not used to people being nice. Most of the time, people just want something from me. A new hit song, an in at the next hot party, publicity. Deron doesn't seem to want anything other than to help me.

"Next house, then? It's only a forty-minute drive from here," he says, and I nod, ready to get going. The water is cooling down, and I'd much rather be in the comfort of my tub at home filled with warmer water and fresher salt. "Buckle up."

Early in the evening, we pull up to a nice neighborhood with two-story houses and wraparound porches. The sun is descending, painting the background sky in pigments of red, purple, and orange. It casts a glow on the car as Deron pulls into the driveway, and I immediately duck down into the water to avoid being seen by any prying eyes. The van has tinted back windows, but I still worry someone might be able to peer inside and see me.

"I'll be back," Deron says. "Try to keep your chin up. We'll get it."

I don't necessarily believe him, but I've also come to terms with what it would mean if we didn't get the pearl back. Deron might not be okay with it to begin with, but he'd find something to do for work eventually. He has to be talented in some way, he just hasn't discovered it yet. I'm sure there's something.

As for me, it wouldn't be that bad to return to the ocean. I miss my dad and siblings a lot, even the sea witch, who's much nicer than you would think. But I would miss performing in front of people the way I can on land. There's something about the acoustics here that makes me sound so much better. Plus, there's the whole "sirens' call" thing that makes all my music irresistible, so I have that going for me.

When several minutes pass and Deron hasn't returned, I start to get a little worried. The water is almost icy now, and it's not as comfortable as it could be. The scales on my legs have grown to their full size, and my voice echoes sometimes when I talk. Whatever time I had is starting to run out, and I'm not even comfortable while it's happening.

In my bag, I hear my phone start to vibrate. It's probably Mr. Rogers again, wondering where I am and why I can't talk. It's been three days—he's probably having a stroke since I haven't returned any of his calls. If I keep it up, he's going to drop me.

It's that thought that makes me answer his call. "Hello?" I say into the phone, and my voice has a tinny note to it.

There's silence on the other line for a moment. Then, "Cassidy? Is that you?"

"Yes."

Another silence. "Wow," Mr. Rogers says. "I—well, to be frank, you sound terrible. I had no idea you were that sick. No wonder you haven't answered my calls."

"I feel terrible," I say, playing into the lie. "I haven't felt up to talking to anyone except Deron."

"Right, Deron," Mr. Rogers says. "Hopefully he hasn't been stressing you out with any events you're missing."

I wrack my brain to think if there were any events besides the *Vogue* photoshoot that I missed, but I can't think of any. There probably were a lot but I'll never know now.

"No, he's been surprisingly helpful," I say.

"That's good," Mr. Rogers says. "I was worried I'd have to have a stern talk with him."

A stern talk would likely scare Deron into the next century, so I'm glad we can avoid that.

"Do you think you'll be ready to perform by this weekend? Saturday, specifically? The late-night talk show wants to have you on board and the record company thought you could perform your new single. It could be a sneak peek, and then we drop it on Sunday. Thoughts?"

This weekend is only two days away. Even if Deron found my pearl necklace today, there's no telling if the side effects would wear off by then. I can't go live with scales on my legs and webbed fingers. The world wouldn't know what to do.

"I may have to take a rain check," I say. "Even if I feel better, there's no way to know whether my voice will be fine to sing or not."

Mr. Rogers seems to consider this, judging by the humming from the other line. "Well, we don't want to risk your voice since you have a tour coming up. I won't tell them one way or another whether you'll be ready, how's that? Then you can let me know Saturday morning how you feel, and we can play it by ear. If you feel fine, it'll be a nice surprise for you to make it to the studio to perform. If not, then we'll still drop the single on Sunday and see how it goes."

"That works for me," I say, coughing to emphasize how sick I am.

I look down at the phone to see how long I've been on the line with Mr. Rogers, and I start to worry about Deron. He's taking awfully long in there. Hopefully nothing happened to him. Should I go in and see? But I don't want to ruin any ground he's established.

Mr. Rogers croons as if to empathize with how I'm feeling. "You rest up and feel better soon, okay? I'll touch base with you on Saturday morning."

"Sounds good. Thanks, Mr. Rogers."

"Take care, Cassidy." He hangs up, and I breathe a sigh of relief.

He believed that I'm still sick (which I am), and I've bought myself two more days before I have to talk to him again. Maybe by then, Deron will have located the necklace. And I won't have scales on my legs anymore.

The sun has completely set and it's dark all around by the time Deron comes out of the house. He closes the front door behind him, pausing on the porchway. I have to strain my eyes to see him since it's so dark, but I can't tell the expression on his face. As he walks to the car, his face is cast downward. It doesn't look like he's holding anything, and I feel my heart sink in my chest. Even though I'd resigned myself to returning to the ocean, I had so been hoping it was taking a long time in there because he had found it.

He slides into the driver's seat and looks back at me. I can't read anything from his facial expression, and his eyes don't give anything away.

Then he rummages in his pocket, sliding out a gold chain with a pearl hanging on the end of it.

"Is this the right one?" he asks. "It was really tough to get back."

As soon as Deron pulled the pearl from his pocket, I could feel a shift in my physical body. Everything in the world felt righted, like it had been tilted on an axis but now was evened out.

He extends the necklace to me, and I waste no time putting it around my neck. The results aren't immediate, but I can feel the shift in my blood. It's only a matter of time before the scales retreat and there's no more webbing between my fingers and toes.

"How did you do it?" I ask. I need to know.

He shrugs. "I promised him front-row tickets for the rest of his life. No backstage passes, though, since he can't be trusted with your things. He also wants a signed poster and you to dedicate your next performance to him."

"That sounds easy enough," I say, relieved Deron didn't have to do anything awful to get the necklace back. Honestly, it sounds a little too easy.

Deron smiles, and that's when I notice a blooming bruise around his right eye. Before I can comment on it, he asks, "Ready to get back to normal?"

By Saturday, the scales have receded and there's no webbing between my appendages. My legs are no longer itchy, and I don't have to spend my entire day inside a salt bath. The pearl is heavy against the base of my neck, but it's a welcome weight.

I put the final touches on that song I'd been writing and get it ready to send to Mr. Rogers. Maybe it'll be my next single.

Deron shows up early that morning, ready to take me to the studio to rehearse. I've already talked to Mr. Rogers and told him I'm good to go, and he seems happier than ever. I didn't realize how much my career affected other people, and it makes me grateful to have my talents back. A lot of people would've lost their jobs, or at least a big portion of their jobs, if I had called it quits and gone back to the ocean.

I'm forever grateful to Deron for getting my necklace back—it couldn't have been easy, and his face is proof of that. So I ignore his sweating problem this morning, and the fact that he forgot about a press conference yesterday.

"Ready, Cassidy?" he asks, for once not correcting himself by calling me *Ms. Mare.*

"Almost," I say. "I have something I want to play for you. It's a song

I'd started writing a few months ago, but I couldn't figure out how to make it personal. Then this morning, I figured it out."

Deron blinks, apparently taken aback. He had his hand on the doorknob but closes the door and follows me to my living room. All of my instruments are here, and I go to the piano for this. It will provide the right sound I want.

While I play, Deron is completely silent. He says nothing; it doesn't even look like he's breathing. He just stands still as a statue in the middle of my living room with his hands shoved into his pockets.

By the time I'm done, my hands are shaking. It's the most intimate song I've ever played, all about first loves and tentative touches. But it's not the lyrics that make it special, it's the charged emotion behind the words.

"That was beautiful," Deron says. "And I'm not just saying that because you're a siren and it's impossible for me to think otherwise. It was really gorgeous."

"I wrote it for you," I say, feeling empowered by his reaction. Reaching out, I grab ahold of his hand. I enjoy the warmth from his palm, and the small smile that accompanies it.

"I'm really lucky," he says, and he squeezes my hand.

His fingers are sweaty, but I don't mind. In fact, I kind of like it.

If you enjoyed this inaugural short story collection from Kaleidascope Author Co-op, check out our winter celebration collection, due for publication December 19, 2023.

 @KaleidoscopCoOp

 facebook.com/kaleidoscopeauthors

 @KaleidoscopeCoOp

 @KaleidoscopeCoOp

Kaleidoscope
Powerful Women
Powerful Writers
Powerful Words

Meet the authors of
Kaleidoscope Author Co-Op

- Madeline Dau -
- R.A. Krueger -
- Chelsea M. Brown -
- Katharine Bost -

Madeline Dau

With her background in healthcare, Madeline Dau enjoys explor-
ing characters that wield fantastical versions of medicine. When
she's not writing, she's running, with grand plans to complete a
half marathon in every state. Her short stories have appeared in
anthologies compiled by Air and Nothingness Press, Lost Boys
Press, and Zombies Need Brains. She resides in Florida with her
family and two of the laziest corgis in existence.

Find her online at madelinedau.com or on Twitter.

 @Madeline_Dau

R.A. Krueger

R.A. Krueger writes Speculative Fiction, usually with a healthy dose of absurdism and a lot of food. She has never heard a pun she didn't like, and she is certain that her humor is wasted on her family. She is a homeschooling mama, a retired pastry chef with an insatiable sweet tooth, and a lover of fabric and sewing. Obsessively planning is her favorite procrastination technique as well as her greatest superpower. If you enjoy badly filmed content, you can find her over on TikTok sharing bits and pieces of writing, reading, and anything else that catches her interest, which usually includes books, sometimes zombies, and always dragons.

 @RAKrueger1   facebook.com/RAKrueger1

 @r.a.krueger.author

Chelsea M. Brown

Chelsea M. Brown writes technical documentation by day and fiction by later day. After completing a bachelor's degree in English from Jacksonville University, she studied fiction writing and publishing at the University of Southern Mississippi. Her novel, *The Order between Sisters*, was published in 2014, and her short stories have been published on *Mystery Tribune* and *The Yard: Crime Blog*. The first chapter of her as-of-yet-unpublished spy novel was on the Voyage YA Journal's Best Chapters Contest longlist. She spends her free time meeting with friends, playing with her dog, and reading, watching, and telling stories about spies, secret societies, and treasure hunting.

 @spies_r_us   facebook.com/spiesrusauthor

 @spies_r_us   @spies_r_us_author

Katharine Bost

Katharine Bost holds an MFA in creative writing from Miami University, and her work has appeared in *Last Resort Literary Review*, *The Doctor T. J. Eckleburg Review*, *Tangled Locks Journal*, and *Mikrokosmos*, among others. She has also been nominated for a Pushcart Prize by *Glassworks* Magazine. If she's not writing, she's either running or begging her cat to stop eating plastic.

 @katharinebost

www.ingramcontent.com/pod-product-compliance
Lightning Source LLC
Chambersburg PA
CBHW022131170626
46808CB00002B/948